FULL CIRCLE

*The elite thought their secrets were safe
—until one voice refuses to stay silent.*

CLAUDETTE MCLENNON

EXPLORA BOOKS
700 – 838 West Hastings St. Vancouver, BC V6C 0A6
www.explorabooks.com
Phone: (604) 330 6795

ISBN: 978-1-997587-59-0 (*Paperback*)
978-1-997587-58-3 (*Hardback*)
978-1-997587-60-6 (*eBook*)

FULL
CIRCLE

Dedication

To my mother, Lileth Rose McLennon, who was my greatest teacher on how to live, how to be, how to be resilient, and how to navigate life's slippery slope. How to think and be a decision-maker, and walk the thin line between love and obsession. She taught how to love God, love honestly, and forgive. And I still miss you. To all my family and friends, thank you for your belief, love, and encouragement.

Acknowledgement

To my faithful supporters and well-wishers, my gratitude to you is boundless. Thank you for always cheering me on and always being in my corner. Your support is felt, and you are appreciated more than you can ever imagine. Thank you also for your patience and understanding.

Table of Contents

Preface

Clarice Boundbrooke—divorced, mother of two—lives in Port Charlotte. She relocated from Mobile, Alabama, when barely out of her teens. She married Barry Gavin Radieux, but they divorced due to Barry's infidelity with a twenty-two-year-old woman. They have two children. They are Maryanne and Felix. Maryanne was gang-raped by her own classmates, members of the football team. People know more than they are saying and will not testify against the pillars of the community's children; the chief of police's son, the manager of Toast Bank, Congressman Forrest Andy Forke and the owner of Busch Auto-dealership and garage. The one witness was "the town drunk" who became the victim of a hit-and-run accident. Evidence had disappeared—clothes, tests, and test results. There was division at school, in the community, and which had found its way even in the Catholic Church.

Chapter 1

"Ladies and gentlemen of the jury, on the count of rape in the second degree, how do you find?"

"Not guilty!"

"On the count of aggravated assault, how do you find?"

"Not guilty!"

"On the count of sexual assault, how do you find?"

"Not guilty!"

"On the count of sexual battery, how do you find?"

"Not guilty!"

After the second not guilty, Maryanne heard the disembodied voice not guilty from a distance. *Not guilty! Not guilty? Not guilty* reverberated in her head. How could this be. On all four counts, it was not guilty! Maryanne opened her mouth and closed it and opened her mouth and closed it again. She was catching her breath. They were guilty. DA Branson held her hand and passed her water, urging her to sip. Her chest heaved, and the advocate Denise Sillas was telling her to breathe slowly and take deep breaths. There was a rushing sound in her ears, and a strangled sound tore from her throat and exploded in "Noooo," and she slumped forward.

She woke in strange surroundings; faces swam in her vision. They all looked like fish to her. Their eyes were odd, bulging, and their movements were jerky. And what was that light? She heard sounds that didn't make sense. She struggled to understand what was going on around her, then decided it was too much and closed her eyes. The second time Maryanne opened her eyes, she saw the form of someone standing by the glass partition. She cleared her throat, and the figure came toward her.

"Oh baby! I'm so glad you are awake."

Maryanne blinked. Her eyes roamed the room. There were *Star Trek* things around her. Was she in the hospital and why? What was she doing here? Her eyes finally focused on the person in the room.

It was her mother, Clarice.

"You gave us such a scare," her mother said.

"A scare? What are you talking about? Where am I? What is happening? Can I have some light?" she asked. Her mother pulled the screen and turned on the light. Her mother kissed her cheek, her forehead, and her hand, now murmuring over and over how happy she was that she was awake finally. Maryanne suffered through the affection like a kitten being washed by its mother.

"Mother, what am I doing in the hospital?"

Her mother explained that the trial was over and that the four young men—Chad Broome, Griffin Spoolson, Caldren Forke, and Matthew Busch—were free. They were found not guilty, and at that, she had screamed, gasped a number of times, then lost consciousness. That was a day ago. She was restless and agitated, and Doctor Rowe thought it best to keep her and sedate her. She ended by asking Maryanne how she was feeling. Maryanne absorbed the information, and slowly it came back to her. Tears were running down her cheeks—hot, scalding tears. How could they. How come the jurors didn't believe her; did they believe she raped herself? How could she. She didn't have a penis; she would not punch herself in the eye with such force that it broke the orbit. She is right-handed, for heaven's sake. Did she punch herself in the left eye? Did she cross-punch for what purpose.

To sport a drooping lid as some form of a trophy? How did life go so wrong? One moment she was looking forward to prom and June graduation. She had applied to Duke University in Durham, NC, and was hoping for a scholarship.

She had also applied to Brown University, Kaiser University, the University of Florida, and Florida State University.

"It's okay, baby. We will make it. You did nothing wrong. You are not a criminal. Evil knows no bounds. It stalks and it preys! Mankind is desperately wicked, but time will take care of them. They will wither and fade, my darling. They robbed you of your name and innocence, but you will rise. Don't cry, baby. It is unfair but you will live to look them in the face, strong and unapologetic. God will see us through this."

Maryanne didn't respond. She thought irreverently about where he was when she was being raped, but she did not verbalize this. She clung to her mother, wishing that this was a nightmare and would be over soon, that she would wake up and be at work at Greeley's Restaurant. Marian asked her mother again to explain why she had been hospitalized. Her mother explained after the not-guilty verdict, she collapsed and was hysterical and had passed out in court. She was taken to the hospital and was so agitated and hysterical that she was sedated to calm her. They were concerned for her safety and well-being due to the earlier trauma and subsequent hospitalization. Maryanne wondered if she was now being viewed as a nut. Well, she had bragging rights now for hitting rock bottom. She could feel dejection calling. For all these months she had kept herself going, believing the four monsters would be jailed. Fifteen years to life seemed like justice. She needed to survive and finish school, even if she could not go to prom. Her thoughts were halted as Dr. Rowe entered the room.

He addressed her, asking if she had a headache, nausea, or dizziness. She told him she felt okay and asked when she could go home. He told her that she had given her mother a scare. He asked about her appetite and if she was paying attention to her food groups. She nodded. He looked into her eyes and looked at her fingernails. He told her that her blood work showed slight anemia. He told her to get dark green vegetables and iron supplements, but if she takes the supplements, she must eat regularly. He told her if she had issues sleeping to use honey and warm milk; he did not want to prescribe any sleeping aid. She should come back to see him in two weeks.

Chapter 2

Maryanne was happy to be going home, but the Dr. said not before she had something to eat. She was disappointed that she was not leaving immediately but with her mother's help, she showered and dressed. She was a little shaky on her feet, but she made it and was sitting up when a tray was brought in. There was chicken noodle soup, mac and cheese, broccoli, and meatloaf. Maryanne had no appetite, but she knew if she did not eat something, she would never go home. She drank the soup, pecked at the broccoli, and ate a little of the mac and cheese. Nothing would prevent her from going. She was there for two days, even if not two full days, but she wanted privacy. She did not want to be a conversation piece or anyone's cocktail discussion if she could help it. At home she would not get the pitying looks and clicking tongues as they shook their heads.

She asked about her brother Felix and father. Her mother told her they had come earlier but left as she was sleeping. She left the hospital quickly as she felt her resentment rising. She needed to hear some music. She didn't need her thoughts right now. She wished her mother would hurry and start the car. Finally, they drove away with Maryanne reaching for the radio dial. She found a country and western station but did not want to hear the heartbreak songs. She flipped until she heard the voice of John Denver singing "Country Roads." Guess she is doomed for the country scene today. Her mother asked her if she had a special dinner request, and she told her she only wanted to go home and listen to some music. She asked if her dad was visiting. Her mother said that she did not know. Maryanne hugged herself, half dejected. The station went to commercial, and she used great restraint not to yell at the radio. As soon as she reached home, she scurried from the car and bolted through the front door. Felix was home and greeted her with "Hi sis!" She answered him with what she hoped was normalcy and returned his awkward hug. He wanted to know how she was and if she wanted anything. She assured him she didn't and crawled into her bed.

She got her collection of Anne Murray's cassettes and Kenny Rogers' and grabbed her radio cassette player and attached her headphones. She needed complete oblivion from thoughts. She needed peace and lots of it. Now she understands Shakespeare's need for music and the excess of it—the only thing was, this was not love. With the tape's volume up, she will drown the events of the last two days and the whole ordeal from her post-Valentine celebration. She did not even want to speak to anyone in the house now. She was glad her dad was not here when she came home and hoped he would not call. As the music pulsed in her head, she became lost for a while. She was sure it would take a long time for her to fall asleep but was surprised as she drifted off during the second go-round of Anne Murray's sultry crooning. She slept and was unsure whether it was from exhaustion or depression.

She woke in the wee hours with Anne Murray's cassette whirring in her ears. She removed the headphones and turned the cassette off. She had slept for a good ten hours and was glad. Now she was hungry, but food held no appeal for her. What a mess everything was. Her parents divorcing was not easy on her or Felix, for that matter. What's irreconcilable differences? She snorted in disgust. She was sure the person who came up with that had a sour stomach that night or was colicky. And imagine people got paid for that. She tried without success to remember all the colleges she had applied to. She applied to many. She knew she did not get into Duke but knew it was a long shot but had tried anyway. She received a scholarship for Florida State University (FSU) but even though she accepted; she knew she would not go. She could not go. School was for intellectuals and mentally sound people. It required attention, focus, and concentration. She did not want to make a mockery of education.

She began to sob. She wanted to be strong; she wanted to fight. She did not want to be a victim, but the echo of the foreman's *not guilty* reverberated in her head over and over. They did not believe her that she had been raped and could identify at least two of the voices. Yes, she blacked out part of the time during that horrendous ordeal, but she remembered the glint of their eyes but more so the voice. She will never forget Chad, as he forced himself in her and the pain that shot through her body. She fought back, raking her fingers across his left cheek. And that's when he punched her in the eye. His partner Griffen asked, "Why you do that for man?"

He said, "The bitch scratched me!" She did not hallucinate, as the defense attorney said. He conceded she could've heard the words but due to the traumatic experience could not identify his client with any degree of certainty, that the voice could belong to anybody. He was right up there with her rapists, maybe one himself.

Why? What did she do to deserve such treatment? She repented of her thoughts that no one should endure what she had. It is so unfair! The rape kit disappeared or was contaminated, they said. The DNA taken from under her fingernails vanished; her underwear and dress got mixed up and misplaced in the evidence room. And to top it off, the one person outside of Dr. Rowe who would testify on her behalf; the day before, was hospitalized due to a hit-and-run accident. Despite this, it was believed that they would be convicted. The support of the advocate from the Rape, Abuse & Incest National Network (RAINN) was invaluable. She was very encouraging, telling her to stay positive. She arranged for her to see a psychiatrist and prepared her for the upcoming court case. She told her what to expect from the defense attorney. (However, nothing could've prepared her for the venom, condescension, and viciousness of that attorney.) She told her to take deep cleansing breaths, have a glass or bottle of water to sip throughout. She was glad for the support, but even Denise Sillas' optimism and caution could not prepare her for a jury so insensitive. They were bought.

She remembered reading that the British believed in and used voice recognition over fingerprints. From the voice they traced nationality, the area one was born, and the school he attended. Chad tried to change his voice. There was an affectation present that was not there before, but the inflection on the words *bitch* and *hit* was unmistakably his. She would not be shaken on that point. And eight stitches later, and burning and pain for weeks, elicited no justice for her. She really wanted to pay them back. This was no fantasy. This was reality. She was raped, and parents and friends supplied them with alibis, phony alibis. They taunted her—making kissing motions to her. Griffen and Matthew even came to say they were sorry she was raped; as if they were not the culprits. She was terrified and shaking; she lunged at them with her pen.

"You slime! She spat at them. Filthy, oily rapists stay away from me. Both your mothers, fathers, and grandparents are pimps. It's in your genes; that's your legacy."

She went back to school at the beginning of May. She stayed low-key just going to the bathroom and back to her class or sitting outside on the bench. She seemed to have leprosy so far; her classmates were concerned. There were the hastily averted eyes, the furtive looks and the cleared path as she walked down the hall. With the exception of Renee and Yolanda, the only two who called and visited her in the hospital after the rape. She was isolated. She spent five days in the hospital for her eyes. She had to have stitches and other bruises and cuts from wrestling with her rapists.

Maryanne began to rock back and forth. The images were too stark. She needed them blurred. They hurt too much.

She wondered for the umpteenth time what drives men to rape. She heard of women too, but more often men were the rapists. Do they plan this, or is it opportunistic? It did not matter but that member that caused such offence should be. She stopped her thoughts. However, thoughts intruded. Didn't the Bible allude to it? Whatever offends! Life sure is a doozy. How could a day born with such promise turn out to be a doozy? She was happy. She had a date with Rutherford. She went over the day again.

Maryanne patted her hair in place and colored her lips with Sassy Pink Lip-gloss. Her blue and white dress flattered her color and hair. She used her Estee Lauder body spritz. It has a flowery scent, perfect for this time of year. It is February, and the weather is pleasant, but could become cool at night. Few people realize that Florida is not scorching hot year-round. She would take her light jeans jacket with her. She was excited because they started dating just before Thanksgiving. They both worked on Valentine's Day and had planned their own celebration for the following Saturday. They were going by Crestview Hills; a beautiful lookout point that overlooked Port Charlotte in the Bay. It had a spectacular view and was a popular spot for high school students. There was an outcrop that offered shelter from the elements, a grass plateau with tall oaks that formed a canopy. It was a great place for a picnic.

At a full moon, the spot was idyllic. Rutherford picked her up at 4:30 p.m. that Saturday. She was so elated at spending a whole evening alone with him, even though she had to prepare their meal.

There was fried chicken, coleslaw, macaroni salad, ham, cheese, crackers, grapes, and strawberries. Because of the onion in the salad, she added a small bottle of scope mouthwash. She chuckled at the mouthwash, telling herself she had to be practical. Romance and onions? No! The two do not go together. They drove to the spot overlooking the town. It was still light, but she wanted to see when the town came to life. She had watched it last December, and it was breathtaking. It was like a symphony, the way the lights went on in the houses and the businesses came aglow as darkness descended. She wondered if it would be the same. She brightened because maybe she'd see the sunset this time. She could see everything.

They parked, and Rutherford spread the blanket on the grass while she got out the white felt back plastic tablecloth and placed wine coolers along with the glasses. She put the fruits and crackers out but hesitated about the cheese. She did not want ants there too soon.

They sat, and Ford opened the wine coolers, and they toasted their love, friendship, and future. They sipped and fed each other the fruits dipped in their drinks. At a point they crossed hands and drank from each other's glasses. They were having fun. The radio cassette player was on, not loud or intrusive but as background to set the mood—Anne Murray did a great job. There was no hurry. They walked to the outcrop. Rutherford had his arms around her waist and rested his chin on her head.

"You look marvelous," he whispered. She twisted her head toward him and was rewarded with a kiss. They stood close in companionable silence. She closed her eyes and could hear Eric Clapton's "Wonderful Tonight." She swayed to the melody in her head. He instinctively started to sway with her. They were content. He nuzzled her cheek and neck, and it was okay. She leaned back even closer. When he turned her around, pulled her from the edge of the outcrop, she did not object, and he kissed her deep and long. She felt goose pimples.

Oh, I'm in love, she thought. They locked in an embrace for a long time, and the shadows stayed at bay. Both returned to the blanket, and then he told her he had a surprise and was going to get it.

Rutherford walked toward his truck parked under some trees. She hummed to herself as she unpacked. Then she wondered what if the chicken wasn't tasty, she thought belatedly. Too bad and too late. Well, she never promised she was a cook, but the love and care that went into the preparation were more than adequate to please his palate. Her back was turned to the truck, and she called out to Rutherford, asking if he needed her muscles. When he did not answer, she turned, and that was when the figure with the mask attacked her. There were four figures, and one clamped his hand over her mouth. He wore a ring with a skull. She tried to twist away, but four against one was a puny contest. Where was Rutherford? She tried to call for help, but the hand muffled the sound. Two held her feet as one got on top of her. Her dress was hoisted, almost obscuring her face. Her black lace underwear was ripped from her body, and she was exposed. Cruelly he forced himself into her. She felt herself tear, and tears ran down her cheeks. She tried to fight, but King Kong's quads were too strong for her. She must've briefly lost consciousness because next she heard him grunt and rolled away.

As another one got on top of her, she stayed quiet, wishing the nightmare would end. When the third one got on her, they believed the fight was gone from her, but she managed to rake his left cheek. He punched her in the left eye. Her vision blurred, but she heard a voice ask, "What you do that for?"

The voice! The one on top her replied angrily, "The bitch scratched me!"

That voice, she knew it! But she was hurting so badly. Her insides felt as if on fire. The fourth raped her too. She tried to mentally distance herself from reality. She was bleeding from her genitals and her eye was bleeding too although she did not realize it then. She didn't know how long she lay there when she heard Rutherford's hoarse voice calling her. He was dirty, disheveled, and unsteady on his feet. "Oh my God, Maryanne! What happened to you?"

His voice caught on a sob. "I am so sorry, so sorry. Those dogs. Those filthy swine!" He was white and shaking. He looked at her shame and raccoon eyes, the cornea partially covered with red. He hugged her, repeating over and over how sorry he was. "I should've protected you," he lamented. Just like that, her world was shattered. Rutherford said he was attacked from behind. Someone grabbed him in a wrestler's chokehold, and a sack was put over his head. The men wore masks, though unsure of their identity, she heard a voice say, "Lay him out cold."

He was hit on the head. He was tied with his belt to a tree. He was on his side and twisted and pulled until he broke the buckle, then removed the sack from his head. Still dazed, he found Maryanne. There were red, angry welts on his neck. The upper arms were bruised and red. In his head, he was thinking, *Got to get you to the hospital.* He gathered her in his arms and stumbled to his truck. When they got there, two tires were flat. Ford swore, uttered some expletives, and kicked the tires.

"We got to get you to the hospital, but the bastards punctured the truck." He became even more incensed. No this cannot be! His spare was at the garage where he worked. He decided to rim it. No choice, has to drive on the flat tires. He would coast down the hill, and maybe they could get help, or he'd make it the three miles or so to the hospital. So, they coast to the main road. Cars and trucks zipped by, ignoring the young man waving. He ran into the middle of the street, trying to wave them down. After a while, Rutherford gave up and drove to the hospital. He did not see one cop or sheriff, no law enforcement officer. He drove to the ER of Brunson Hospital on Honway St. He went to the ambulance entrance with his hand on his horn. No one came running. He realized that only happened in the movies. He ran into the ER and returned what seemed like a year later with two nurses with a gurney. He eased her slowly and tenderly out of the front seat.

As the nurse saw the swollen, blackened eyes almost closed, the nurse demanded to know what had happened. He explained that they were attacked by a gang of men while out on a date. The men wore masks and unsure of their identity, but remembered the voice saying, "Lay him out cold." At the saying, the man's arms tightened around his neck, and he was hit on the head, and a bag was put over his head.

He hung his head in embarrassment and regret.

"I didn't protect her," he said forlornly.

The nurses hurriedly placed her on the gurney and took off shouting, "Coming through." Rutherford ran after them. He kept clearing his throat, maybe from earlier pressure, and for the first time his throbbing head registered. Inside, everything was a blur, and she heard everyone from a distance. She heard Rutherford say she was raped and was hit by one of the rapists. Voices swirled around her.

"Poor thing. Those animals!"

"Those S.O.B! Oh, dear God! What a horror."

Her next awareness was a doctor standing over her, stating, "Take it easy. I'm not going to hurt you. Nurse get in here."

She could see a pale green screen. She heard rape kit and the doctor's strained voice saying, "It doesn't get any easier dealing with a rape victim because I can do nothing to console the person or fix it."

"I feel impotent," he added. She started to cry for her mother and was told she was on the way. The next she knew she was in a large room with persons with covered heads and noses. She became agitated and started to shout. A nurse came to her and told her she had had minor surgery and in a day or two would see if she would need additional surgery for her fractured orbital eye. An assessment would be done after the CAT scan was seen by an ophthalmologist. She was told she was going to the floor and her parents were waiting there.

Her parents met her on the second floor. "Mom," she sobbed even with the anesthesia still present. She reached for the comfort of her mother. Her mother hugged her, and her father came and kissed the top of her head.

"Hey there, kitten. Oh, my baby, I wish I could get my hands on those bastards."

She felt strange. She was nauseous and asked for a basin; she needed to vomit. There was no nurse in the immediate area, and her mother grabbed a basin from next door. She vomited, and then the nurse came. Her mother asked for a cup so she could rinse her mouth. She realized she had a catheter then, and she started to cry all over again. While her mother moved away to discuss the catheter, her father sat on her bed, hugging her.

"I'm so sorry. As your dad, I wish I could take away your pain, kitten. Is Rutherford trustworthy? How did they know you were there?"

"I don't want to talk about it. Where is he, anyway?"

"The last I knew they were trying to get him to submit to an examination of his head. He wanted to be with you," he said.

Her mother returned and explained that the catheter was necessary for her comfort, as the uric acid and stitches would be most uncomfortable. Maryanne got the information halfheartedly. She was so nauseous. Her mother told the nurse who offered Mylanta and ordered herbal tea to try to settle her stomach and stem the nausea. Maryanne knew she would not be drinking any tea. They taste horrible for the most part with very few exceptions. She hoped by some miracle she'd get peppermint. When she voiced this and her mother started to rummage through her bag. There was very little her mother could not find in her bag, she thought, amused.

Surprisingly the water was hot when it came, and her mother produced not only peppermint but lemon zinger as well.

Maryanne smiled and said, "Good job, Mom."

The parents laughed along with Maryanne. Maryanne looked at them. They were seldom in accord anymore. They divorced eight years ago, and her mother has custody of Felix and herself. They rotated the major holidays. Her paternal grandparents, Ira and Pullar Radieux did not visit much since the divorce. Maryanne and Felix liked spending time with them. They were cool as grandparents and lots of fun. They would go fishing and watch the Port Charlotte minor league baseball team. They would take them to the zoo in Naples and Punta Gorda. The zoo in Naples was huge and always colorful and exciting. She sighed inwardly. She was sorry about the divorce. It was hard on Felix. He wanted to be with his dad so badly. For a while, there were almost daily reports from his class teacher. Once the school knew of the divorce, they got him to speak with the guidance counselor. They invited their father to meet with them. It helped.

Maryanne turned back to sipping her tea when two uniformed officers came to her. They introduced themselves as PO Mazzelli and Powell. They wanted statements of the rape. They had already spoken with Mr. Wood. Her father told them she was still suffering aftereffects of the anesthesia and asked them to come back. However, they can confer with the doctor. The doctor came, looked at her, and said her eyes looked glazed, and perhaps they'd get more from her the next day. They left, wishing her goodnight. Shortly after, Maryanne fell asleep. She woke once in the night and found herself groaning in pain. The IV was twisted, so it was hurting her hand as well as her delicate part; it was hurting fiercely, as well as her left eye. She was a mass of pain. The catheter was a burden. She pressed the bell, and the nurse came and gave her pain medication. She could not stop the tears. Whatever the nurse gave her, it worked like magic. She slipped into a deep sleep. Or, because her body was not accustomed to medication, it knocked her out. She realized why persons complain you never rest in the hospital.

At an ungodly hour of the morning, it was vitals and an hour after that medication, all before 7:00 a.m. The next time she woke, the clock showed 10:00 a.m. She looked at the breakfast, now cold, beside her on the table. Her mother's face swam into view. She blinked and saw the nurse and another lady. The nurse introduced herself as her nurse for today, and Ms. Brooks was the SW. Both ladies spoke in a soft voice, and when asked, Maryanne said she wanted her mother there with her. The SW gently expressed sympathy for her ordeal, then gently probed about her injury. She informed her about counseling and about the Rape, Abuse & Incest National Network (RAINN) that will provide an advocate who will assist her through the court process and trial ordeal. There were other services, both medical and social service avenues, open to rape victims. They left shortly afterwards.

Soon after she finished drinking her peppermint tea, then PO Mazzeli and Detective Powell arrived. After securing permission from her, they asked her to recount the events of the evening before. She told them about her date with Rutherford Wood. They were going on a picnic date to celebrate Valentine's Day. They could not go the week before because she had to work. He picked her up at 4:20 p.m. and drove them to Crestview Hills. It was a short drive, but they wanted to be there to enjoy the sunset. They wanted to be eating by sunset, feasting on fried chicken, coleslaw, macaroni salad, cheese, and Bartles & Jaymes wine coolers. They ate the cheese and crackers, strawberries, and grapes before their meal. They used disposable wine glasses, making believe it was champagne. They linked their arms and fed each other. The sun was going down, and the orange glow spread across the sky. They could see the colors blending: the purple, the pinkish flush, the amber and burnish orange. It was beautiful; Earth at its best. Her face mirrored the pleasure and contentment of the scene. Her voice trailed almost to a stop. It was then Rutherford told her he had a surprise for her and headed for his truck where they had parked. She was rearranging the food on the white-and-red tablecloth when she called out to him. She wondered what was taking him so long and if he needed her help to lift whatever it was. He did not answer, but she did not think anything of it. Her back was turned as she looked at the sunset. She heard a sound, turned to greet Rutherford, and that's when she saw four men in masks. She was about to ask, "Who are you?" when one of the men threw her to the ground. She was winded when she fell, and he followed her down and proceeded to hold her down.

She twisted and moved as much as she could, and he asked the others to hold her legs. By this her voice was dead, flat. Pain etched on her face. The detectives noticed her protective stance and knew she was reliving the horror, but they had to get the details.

They taunted, "Your lover boy is not going to help you. He's busy-sorta tied up. You can't expect a boy to do a man's job. So enjoy this. It's the best you are ever gonna get."

She started to scream for Rutherford, then for help. The fourth held her hands above her head. The ringleader then lifted her dress, ripped her underwear off, and raped her. First one, then the other. She screamed, and the one raping her put his hand over her mouth, and that's when she saw a ring, maybe silver and looking like a skull. They took turns raping her, and while the third one was raping her, she was hurting so badly, but anger rose in her and she started to fight him. She scratched his cheek at the jawline. He screamed and punched her in the left eye. His partners asked, "Why you do that for?"

And he replied, "The bitch scratched me."

She believed she blacked out because the next she knew she felt fingers rubbing her mons pubis. He then raped her.

Det. Powell closed his eyes. He cannot imagine the pain this young woman was in. He felt the gun in his holster.

Dear God, he prayed, *let me be a cop and not a vigilante* because he felt like finding them and administering justice. He pulled a shaky breath.

"I am so terribly sorry for your ordeal. No one should ever be raped or subjected to it."

Maryanne nodded, tears flowing freely like the water flows after a deluge.

"Are you okay. Do you want us to leave?" asked Det. Mazzeli. As Maryanne shook her head, he said he had to ask what he used to rape and penetrate her.

She was shocked, angry, and upset by the question. "Sure, lay it on. Yeah, go ahead. Kill me, why don't you? Maybe I would be better off dead, anyway."

He explained that they needed to know specifically, as any object could be used, not that it changed the crime. She told them no object but their penises. By this she was crying openly. Her mother told them it was enough. PO Powell asked if she knew the attackers. She started to shake her head, then remembered the voice of the one that had hit her. She knew the voice! She told them she knew the voice of the one that hit her, Chad Broome. And the first voice was Griffen Spoolson. She knew the voice. The third one had auburn hair and a mole on his upper lip.

Fear, shame, and disgrace followed her around; she felt dirty and unclean. She could not shake the guilt of what had happened. Maryanne came back to the present. The rape had changed her relationship with Rutherford. She didn't blame him, although he blamed himself. Matthew Busch invited him to a party that day, and he declined; he had a date. When Matthew asked him where he was going, he told him about the picnic at Crestview Hills. He never gave any other information. He was sure he never suggested that there was any dalliance by word or action. She believed him. It was her shame. She could not forget he saw her at her most vulnerable, torn, raped and bloody.

Rutherford gave strong statements he was jumped from behind and that he had punched one in the gut and should be sporting a bruise as he got him in the solar plexus and another with a jab in the kidney region. He noticed the ring on the attacker's finger, a skull with black eyes, and one wore a brown shoe with metal tips at the toe. The second one that came to help had on an unusual cologne. It was familiar somehow. He had smelled it earlier; the same one Matthew Busch wore. The gorilla-like arms that gripped him he could not break, and he was hit on the head, in addition to the chokehold. He swore it was Matthew and his three pals: Chad Broome, Griffen Spoolson, and Caldren Forke.

Rutherford was convinced of Matthew's guilt. He knew he would deny it but, decided to try anyway. The four boys were each other's alibis. Rutherford asked Matthew if he had told anyone that he was going to Crestview Hills. Naturally he denied it. So, Rutherford knew that he could not tackle Matthew by himself, but he could handle Caldren. He devised a plan to get him alone. He remembered Caldren's car, and fortunately, he had purple paint he could douse the Benz sports car with, which would force him to take it to the Busch garage where he worked to have the paint removed. This had him coming into the garage five days after the rape. Rutherford took the job to remove the paint. When Caldren came to pick up the car, he dared him to pick up an engine that was waiting for repair. It was just a test to see who was stronger. Because he was so egotistical, he accepted the dare. Rutherford watched as Caldren struggled to catch his breath after being unsuccessful in the attempt.

He was very friendly, confessing that he could not pick it up himself; instead, Rutherford showed him how many pull-ups he could do on the BendPak XPR (used to hoist cars) but blindfolded. Like all jocks, he cannot pass up the opportunity to show off. He put the blindfold on and started his count. In the meantime, Rutherford got the portable laser machine used for cleaning metal and rust removal. He pretended to turn the machine on. Because he was doing Caldren a favor, he came after hours when everyone left for the day so, no witnesses. He advanced with strobe lighting and a cassette where he'd recorded the sound of the laser machine removing rust from a car. All this he had set up the day before.

He told Caldren, "I have some questions for you, and you must answer truthfully. I have a machine used to remove rust and will use it on you if I do not get the truth. Do you understand?"

Rutherford then turned on the recorder and the strobe light. The flashing light convinced Caldren to cooperate. Rutherford asked him who raped Maryanne. He stuttered; he didn't know. Rutherford moved closer with the recorder, turning the sound louder, and at that Caldren said Matthew had told them of the date, but they planned only to spook them. Rutherford revved up the second recorder, and he touched his neck with a file and said it would be his offending member next. Caldren started to cry. "Please don't. Don't cut my penis off. Are you crazy? Please! Please!"

He was asked to name his accomplices. He named Mathew Busch, Chad Broome, and Griffen Spoolson. Rutherford wanted to know how it escalated to rape? He said it was Chad and Griffen's idea. They said they were sure there would be sex and wanted to partake of some of what Rutherford was going to get. Said that many people would not be there after Valentine's and it's not yet spring. He said Chad punched Maryanne; Griffen raped her first, then Chad, Matthew, and then him, but he swore he didn't enjoy it. He began to whimper in earnest and beg. Rutherford asked him who jumped him. He said he did, and Matthew hit him on the head with a plank. Just as he was about to hit Caldren, Mr. Busch Sr. entered and wanted to know what was going on.

Chapter 3

Rutherford told him nothing. They were playing a game called bait. "What the hell is going on?" he hollered. He looked around and saw the laser machine-rust remover with the strobe light flashing—not that he noticed it was the strobe.

"Christ, what are you doing. Turn that **** thing off!"

"I can't," said Rutherford quietly.

Reginald Busch moved toward the machine, and Rutherford said quietly. "It is not on," Rutherford showed the cassette recorder and the strobe light. The machine was not plugged in.

"What is the meaning of this? Are you outa your cotton-picking mind?"

"Well, Mr. Busch, sir, I just heard a confession that Chad Broome, Griffen Spoolson, Cal here, and your son Matthew raped Maryanne Radieux, choked and hit me in the head."

"What! You are crazy. Matthew did no such thing. I don't know what this fool said, but it's not true. None of it. My boy had nothing to do with it."

"He confessed!" said Rutherford.

"Did your boy? What made you do a foolish thing like that? You don't have anything good to say, shut the hell up," thundered Mr. Busch. By this time, Mr. Busch was red in the face and breathing hard. He helped Cal down and removed the blindfold.

"Please, Mr. Busch, he threatened to cut off my manhood if . . . if I . . . I," Cal stammered.

"Shut up, you fool." He turned to Rutherford. "You no longer work here. You commit a crime in my place of business to ruin me."

"No, Mr. Busch, your son and his pals committed a crime: rape, sexual assault, and battery. And you lied and gave your son an alibi for the time. You are scum! Playing the upright citizen who goes to mass because you are such a good Catholic, right? Did he learn his values from you? Don't you see? It's all the upright and leading citizens of the town whose sons are rapists."

His words hit the mark. Reginald Busch turned redder, if that were possible. He looked like a beet, and a vein pulsed at his neck. He clenched his fist and moved toward Rutherford, who calmly said, "You can try and make my day," as he widened his stance, borrowing from *Dirty Harry.*

The calmness of his tone, eyes that turned from flint to green, and the low, gravelly voice full of confidence stopped Busch. For the first time he "looked" at Rutherford. That was controlled anger and violence wrapped in one. Even with Cal there, he knew he would be a formidable opponent and he couldn't take him.

"How 'bout you, Cal. Wanna try again with me facing you? See the remnants of the choke still on my neck. Why don't you finish it? Ah! I forget. You only attack from behind when you have company or defenseless girls, and with friends. You sniveling coward. Yellow belly! Chicken! Come on, you are not yellow. Sorry, I missed your name. Rapist."

They squared off, and Rutherford made a jerky movement of his torso, and both put up their hands defensively. Rutherford laughed. He shook his head, laughing, his even white teeth glowing like a Colgate commercial in his angular face.

"So, Busch, all those teenage girls and women you grope, etc. etc.—you sleep easy nights? Is that why you so easily provided an alibi?"

"Get out! Get the **** out and don't darken my doorway ever again, or I'll have you arrested for trespass."

"No need to holler; I'm going. Besides, it stinks—must be all the rape victims clamoring for justice."

Rutherford sauntered out but broke into a run once outside. Armed with the new information, he went to the precinct and asked for PO Mazzeli and Powell. They were out on a call. He left a message that they should call him. It was urgent pertaining to the Maryanne Radieux case and left his number. He went home with his props. He felt sick every time he thought of her ordeal. Why? With all those four have! With the wealth their parents have, the jobs, the so-called prestige in the community, yet they commit so heinous a crime against a lone female. His Maryanne with the sparkling eyes and gorgeous smile. The depraved bastards! They were predators. He wished he could get them alone individually. He was sorry Busch turned up. He was looking forward to beating the crap out of Caldren. He didn't want to get anyone else involved, or else he would pay them back. He would beat them, tie them up, but would be generous and leave them by the side of the road. Belatedly he remembered that he did not look at Cal's stomach. The black and blue would still be there; maybe purple. He couldn't remember the different stages of a bruise, but it didn't matter.

Rutherford desperately wanted the police to call him back before the reprobates could rally and hatch a plot. He hoped pride would hold Caldren's lips, but he knew Reginald Busch wouldn't. It was a race against time. He wanted to tell Maryanne, but he wanted to be home when the cops called, and he did not want to be on the phone in case they called. He was a caged tiger. He paced. He checked his watch several times. The minute hand wasn't working. It had not moved, or so it seemed. Rutherford considered calling his friend Ralph but decided against it. His grandmother called to him to stop turning her carpet into thread. She wanted to know why he was so agitated, whether it was because of the hit on his head last week. Rutherford laughed and told her no. She came from the kitchen with the ever-present apron around her neck.

"Now sit down! Sit down and tell me what got you so riled up like that."

"Well, Grams, today Caldren Forke confessed that he, Chad Broome, Griffen Spoolson, and Matthew Busch, raped Maryanne," said Rutherford.

"Chad, Caldren, and Griffen, who are they? My poor Maryanne. Poor lamb! What a horrendous act. Awful, awful. Just so terrible, and she's such a doll too. I hope they lock them up and throw away the key. What sort of home training do these hooligans get? Just goes to show no good comes of spoiling kids."

"You know, Grams, Chad is the Police Chief's son, Caldren Congressman Andy Forkes' son, Griffen Spoolson Toast Bank Manager's son, and Matthew Busch—Reginald Busch Car Dealership and garage owner, my former employer."

"Oh, dear Lord! How and why. Goodness! All of them from good families. And how did he come to confess?" Gram asked.

"Well," he said sheepishly, with a little friendly persuasion. "I might have tricked him some, but he choked me and raped my Maryanne. She's my girl, Grandma. I am not concerned about me, but he and his scum friends raped Maryanne. Imagine being raped by four men!" Tears ran down his cheeks.

"They cannot get away with it, should not be allowed to get away with it. I went to the precinct, but PO Mazzeli and Powell were out on a call."

Rutherford wiped his cheeks. He got angry every time he thought of the rape. He was glad he had followed his hunch. The cologne, the shoes, the ring, and Matt's knowledge of his date with Maryanne, all added up. Matt bragged about his cologne previously, saying that it was a special blend of pine, orange blossom, smoke, and whatever else he said, but he privately thought he left out skunk-oil.

Grams hugged him. "It is good you looking out for Maryanne, but you didn't get yourself into any trouble, did you?"

"No Grams. I just tricked him into believing he would get hurt if he didn't tell the truth. I am calling the precinct. The wait is killing me."

Rutherford called the precinct, and this time he was in luck. He told the officers he knew who had raped Maryanne and had hit him on the head. They said they'd come by. When they came, he explained how he'd got Caldren to do pushups on the hoist equipment in Busch's Garage blindfolded. He then asked him who had raped Maryanne. He named Chad Broome, Griffen Spoolson, Matthew Busch, and himself. He said Matt told them about the date on Crestview Hills and had planned to spook them, but Chad and Griffen decided to get some of what they thought the Rutherford was going to get. Chad punched Maryanne in the eye. Griffen raped her first, Chad, Matt, then him. He, Caldren, jumped Rutherford, and Matthew hit him with a piece of plank. As he came to the end, he suddenly remembered the tiny tape recorder he had. He removed it from his pocket, having forgotten about it until then.

The officers took notes while he talked and did not stop him. "So, did you hurt this Caldren guy? So, we will find no bruises on him?" they inquired.

They turned the tape recorder on. There was audio, but low. It was audible (but if enhanced, would be heard much clearer). They definitely heard Rutherford ask who raped Maryanne, and Caldren naming the fellows.

"Good work—just hope it will hold up in court," said Mazelli.

Rutherford reminded them to check the stomach for bruises; he was sure it was on Matthew and Caldren.

They took him to the precinct to give his written statement. They left to speak with the sergeant. The chief was out of town at a convention. Rutherford did not know that but was happy they had proof. He wasn't sure what the chief's reaction would be to know his heir was a common convict and a rapist. He could not hear everything, but he heard DA and swearing out warrants for the four rapists. He was told to go home as they needed to find a judge to sign off on the warrants. He'd be brought in when the boys/men were picked up. Rutherford knew then he had done his best to see those bastards imprisoned. He had tried them and found them guilty. Fifteen years to life, according to his research and the lawyer he had asked. Aggravated rape was serious. He wanted them to pay for that assault on Maryanne. She did not deserve that.

Heck, he thought. *No! No! No one deserves to be raped.*

He felt sick all over again as he heard her whimpering as he neared her after he freed himself. He remembered how her body shook and the blood and the violence that hung in the air. He had not cried since ten years old when Bobby Shultz and Greg Steele beat him up on his way from school. But that day he cried. He felt impotent—Maryanne was hurting and he could not help her. The scene played over and over in his head. Rutherford shook his head to dispel the memories. Her mom said she needed surgery for her eye. Beautiful Maryanne with laughing hazel eyes and a thick black mane. She was even more gorgeous when she smiled. She inherited the smile from her mother, but the black hair from her father.

They were decent folks—Maryanne's mother works at the library, and her dad is an insurance broker with AllState— albeit they are divorced, and her father married a much younger woman. But that was no reflection on Maryanne. Yes, they were the ones who got dressed up on Sundays and went to Mass. He did not like his sudden switch of thoughts of church and Mass, so he changed out of his overalls and decided to go for a run. He'd run for about an hour. He would go at marathon pace. He knew after his legs would start burning, but he needed the distraction to keep his mind off retaliation and payback. All he needed was ten minutes with each perp. Only ten minutes! What was the saying revenge is a dish served cold? He didn't know that. With the adrenaline pumping cold didn't fit with him. However, Grams would suffer if he went to jail. She loved him so much.

You win now, boys, he thought. *Thanks, Grams.*

Chad, Griff, Cal, and Matt were arrested. They were placed in a lineup. There were eight men. Everyone was asked to say, "Lay him out cold." The voice was that of Chad. Rutherford identified it with ease, even though it was not behind a mask. The timbre of his voice was unmistakable. It wasn't James Earl Jones or Johnny Gilbert, but easily identifiable. Next, their shoes were examined, and sure enough, the brown shoes with the square metal tip were worn by Caldren. The group was also asked to unbutton their shirts, exposing their torsos. And there was the black and blue that had gone purple with a tinge of yellow due to time and age of the bruise. Caldren and Matthew sported the bruises on their stomachs. They stumbled over their answer about the origin of the bruise. Later Maryanne would need to listen to the voices as well and anything else that would help identify her rapists. The four were held in jail over the weekend.

Rutherford visited the hospital the next day to tell Maryanne the good news. Maryanne was listless but brightened a little. She would want to know everything that happened. He told her about putting purple paint on Calden's car, and he subsequently had to have it removed and restored to its original color at the main garage in town. When he came to pick it up, he challenged him to pushups blindfolded. While Cal was blindfolded, Rutherford got out the strobe light and his radio cassette recorder with prerecorded sounds of the rust removal machine; he turned it on and promised he'd use it on Cal's you-know-what if Cal did not tell the truth. He named his three friends: Chad, Matt, and Griffen. He also had a recording of the admission/confession. For that moment, both felt gratified that the horrible bastards would go away to jail for a long time. They hoped the added violence of the punch in the eye and Greg's statement and interview would seal their fate even if their parents are the so-called pillars of society.

Events progressed after. However, the chief returned from his travels, and things became robust and aggressive as he collared the officers for doing their jobs. With all his years of experience, he didn't have the decency to remove himself from the investigation until pressure from the District Attorney. It's not unusual that he would want to help his son, but if ever there was a need for a clandestine operation, it was now. He knew Marianne and her mother, the whole family, and that was awkward. He failed to even acknowledge what happened. Clarice passed and greeted him, and he scowled without answering. His wife Bethany mumbled. They served on the women's committee, and it got tense and uncomfortable, where the members started to take sides.

Clarice found herself in the minority for the first time. Bethany Busch's money and prestige in the community guaranteed her more cohorts. It was bad enough that she was a divorcee. Clarice was flabbergasted that people she regarded as friends merely nodded and some favored her with plastic smiles. She did not understand. How do you blame a victim of rape? It is such a horrible, hurtful thing to do to anyone. It was strange that the leading ladies avoided her with their over-sprayed hairdos. Whereas previously she was embraced with smooches, now it's quickened steps, averted eyes, an embarrassed laugh or "I didn't see you there, Clarice." The hypocrites! It hurt because these women were her peers, with whom she often discussed their children, shared a new casserole recipe, and reviewed the newest fashion. Now, that camaraderie melted like snow in hot July.

So she was isolated. She was thankful to Beatrice and Joan. They hugged her and were friendly and expressed their regret and offered their shoulders anytime. She looked at the two African American women with gratitude. They knew adversity. They did not take sides. She was glad of their friendship and was glad she had always been cordial to them.

Clarice was happy when she learned there was a witness who could seal the fate of the four boys. She wanted justice for her beloved daughter. Rutherford did well getting the confession, even if it was in an unorthodox way but at least there were faces to the atrocities. It was disturbing that the rapists attended the same school. These so-called high school jocks believed they could do anything and get away with it, including gang rape. There was too much privilege given to some male athletes and coaches, and principals overlooked crimes on the grounds of producing stellar athletes. They got away with beating up students not athletically inclined, all in the name of a state championship. Working as she did, she heard snippets of conversations about the atrocities of these delinquents and infractions that would normally get you expelled were excused.

When the DA told her they had found a witness who could corroborate Rutherford's taped confession, she was extremely glad. They declined to say who it was. They said it was important to keep it quiet; the statement was both verbal and recorded. As the weeks drew closer to the trial, she was nervous and anxious but presented a strong, calm exterior. She had to be strong for Maryanne, poor lamb. Those bastards had turned her happy, positive, gregarious daughter into a sniveling, morose child—the light disappearing from her eyes and with it the joy of living. Her two friends, Renee and Yolanda, tried to cheer her up, likewise Rutherford. He'd lost his job at Busch's Garage but was now working at Lowe's.

Many times she went back to the snippets of conversations she overheard. The gang of four was quarreling, and their lawyer said the confession was forced and therefore there was nothing to be worried about; they were safe. That they have to prove it and the cops could not, even though they brought in outside help. They admonished each other to zip it. Clarice could hardly contain her excitement. She told PO Powell what she overheard and urged them to speak with Linda Eyre and Greta. She didn't know Greta's last name. Later she found out that Linda denied knowing or having information about the four. She decided to face Linda, mother to mother, to plead with her to tell what she knew to the cops. Linda refused, stating that she knew nothing. Clarice told her she overheard her talking with Greta at the diner and repeated verbatim what Linda said. Linda was shocked at the accuracy of Clarice's statement. She blustered that it was only talk, and she was repeating gossip she had heard. She refused to say where she heard the gossip—said it was just talk, people were talking. Linda insisted it was only talk, nothing factual. She said she could not help, even though she was sorry about Maryanne and what an ordeal for the poor child.

"Sure, Linda; you are sorry. The way you kiss Mr. Spoolson's ass, sure you are sorry; but forgive me, I don't know what I expect. You surely are the right height to kiss his derriere; just right. Pray this ordeal is not visited on you, good Catholic that you are."

Clarice was so angry at Linda. Later she thought people don't have to empathize with you. It was not their business. She realized she was seeking compassion. She wondered what she could've done to protect Maryanne. She would've preferred if she were the victim, not her baby. That night she cried herself to sleep. She felt lonely for the first time since her divorce. She hated that bimbo who had invaded her marriage. All the old bitterness came back about her divorce. She knew he was unfaithful to her. She ignored it at first, but the second time she got chlamydia, she had to face it. She was not unfaithful, and chlamydia is transferred through sex only, and she had seen the GYN two weeks prior. The second time she confronted him, she went into the bathroom and saw him grimacing as he peed and complained of pain and burning. He said he had been drinking too much beer and not enough water. She had lower abdominal pain and discharge. Dr. Green gave her antibiotics and told her the male had to be treated too, as it did not go away on its own and she would be re-infected. She told her doctor bluntly that she took her wedding vows seriously and did not play around. Infidelity was not her indulgence. She told Gavin then to go to his doctor and get antibiotics because she knew he had given it to her. After some months, she told him unless he wore condoms, there'd be no sex. She knew he wouldn't agree, but it didn't matter to her. She was not unfaithful to him. Men like Gavin never want to wear condoms. It cramped their style. Well, since he had a mistress, he wouldn't suffer.

One night after a long committee meeting, she saw Gavin's car parked at Chelsea's Grill and Bar. She went in, but he wasn't there. The place wasn't crowded, and she waited ten minutes then left. His car was still there outside. She knocked on the restroom door, but got no response. She bent and looked under the stall and found nothing. He didn't mean it when he said he'd stopped seeing the woman he got the chlamydia from. She wasn't really shocked, but intimacy was over between them. One day she went PTA meeting; and he didn't show up though he promised. On her way home, she saw him with the child—his newest fling. She looked little more than a child to her. It was then that she called PI Drake.

She gave him a picture and the car license number because her health was at stake. She wanted a divorce. The children hardly saw him. He was hardly there. He missed all of Felix's baseball games and Maryanne's dance recitals. He just changed his clothes there. She was tired of making excuses to the children. She never nagged. He slept at the front of the bed with his own covers. She was fine.

A month later, Stan Drake brought her pictures and a tape of her husband's infidelity. The couple frequented Country Inns and Suites, Radisson, 124–244 Corporate Court. They had dinner there twice per week but mostly at her apartment on Beatrix Boulevard. The apartment was hers, rented nine months ago and paid for by Gavin. She didn't know how he got all that information, but she accepted it was legal for a PI. She hid the package in her pocketbook and hid it under her bed. The next day, after the children were safely at school, she decided to watch the videotape.

Clarice gasped! What on earth was that? Sweet Jehoshaphat, what on earth was that girl doing. She was a contortionist. How did she get her body that way? In shock, she watched her husband Gavin standing there in his birthday suit. She had to admit he looked good for a forty-five-year-old man. But she looked again at the young girl and wondered what intimacy had to do with what she was doing. As the young girl continued her performance and Gavin joined in, Clarice knew she would never want Gavin for a husband again. But as if mesmerized, she stared. What that woman was doing lacked decency and dignity. She was no prude, but good lord, what she did with her body was unbelievable. When did making love change so drastically? Apparently, Gavin knew because he was right there with her. She guessed that's what they call "kinky." What her husband and his mistress were doing didn't even look sanitary. She was disgusted, and a wave of nausea washed over her. She pulled the tape out and shoved the package under the bed. She cried for what was and what would not be. There was no happy ever after. The next day she contacted a lawyer and asked Gavin to be home at seven. It was Friday, and the children had a sleepover. She told him that she needed a divorce. He blamed her for denying him conjugal rights; that's why he did it. She listened to him stutter and bluster, then asked him quietly if she had given him chlamydia as well.

She told him she was not moving, and he already has a place at Beatrix Boulevard, and since he is already supporting two households, should not be a hardship for him. He ranted and raved, and she took the tape out and played it for him.

"Oh god. Oh god," he said when he saw himself. "Stop. Stop!"

She obliged. He was to agree to the divorce on the grounds of infidelity, and she would not give it to the court as evidence. She was not the star of that show. She told him to leave anytime, but he must tell his children face to face. Clarice sighed and came back to the present. None offered solace. The past was painful; the present horrible, and the future frightening. *The Lord help us all,* she thought. She made the sign of the cross.

Chapter 4

Clarice, still determined to follow every lead and story, spoke often to Renee and Yolanda. Renee pledged to speak with Chad's girlfriend, Bridgette Street. Bridgette provided Chad with an alibi for the evening of the attack. She allegedly told the cops that he was with her between the hours of 4:30 p.m. and 5:30 p.m. Renee was determined that that dumb blonde would retract her statement. Clarice believed that every bit helped as she was getting no cooperation from the adults, who didn't have amnesia insisted that what they heard was just talk and could not be sure exactly what was said. Yet, she'd get anonymous calls about the rape continuously, or rather taunts, because the person/persons said they were boys from the high school and they wore masks—that they bragged about the rape, how Maryanne begged for more loving. And said all women enjoyed rough sex, that the meek demeanor was for show only and welcomed the roughness.

The person or persons usually hung up very fast. Clarice begged to know the identity and asked the person to tell the police. Another time she heard they were arguing about that evening and their alibis.

She wished she were clairvoyant so she could know all things. She was tired of thinking of ways the four boys would pay for their crime. She'd asked the DA if they'd be charged as adults given the brutality of the crime. Heinous, more accurately described it, she thought in anger. For weeks she followed every scrap of lead. She was sick of hearing "they say," without one person having the guts to confirm what they knew. In her heart she knew these persons were not at Crestview that horrible night, but there was fighting among the four. Yet, mouths were clamped shut. For that reason, she gave beatific smiles and nodded. She could not bear to hear the platitudes. The most or best information she got was from Madeline, the bag lady. Madeline said she overheard Chad, the Chief's boy, say nobody can prove anything. That the scratch on his face would heal. Said pops would fix it. No rape; that was gone. But who would believe her? She believed it, but would the police, the DA? Madeline pushed her shopping cart, carrying her worldly possessions with her. Rumor had it she had lost her mind when her husband ran away with his secretary and their five-year-old son. Gradually she lost her home. She never worked, and by the time she realized what was happening, the house had been repossessed. She was placed in a shelter after she left Calvell Psychiatric Hospital. Madeline claimed she had a visit from Pope John Paul 11 and he told her she would be reunited with her son. She would proudly display a tattered picture of her son Paul—age four. Poor Madeline! Was she so desperate that she believed Madeline? Madeline who operated in a world of her own. Must've heard something she reasoned. She must have. She must have. Her descriptions of the boys were on point. One had brown hair, pretty with a red car; the other walked with swagger and cowboy boots. She told the DA but he said Madeline was impaired and known for seeing and hearing things. Recently she had a visit from the angel Gabriel. Clarice questioned Madeline again if there was anyone else walking when the boys were talking, but she said she did not see anyone else.

She performed her job by rote. There was no joy. She did what they paid her to do. She was heartbroken. Gavin had a new wife, so she could not share her pain and frustration with him. The church was already divided. She was more grateful for Beatrice and Joan, the two Afro-American women. Funny, she trusted them. She knew with sudden certainty that she could confide in them if necessary. It was through them she found out about Greg, the wino. They fed him while trying to get him off the bottle. At one time, a tiler by trade, he did beautiful work for them, and they never forgot. Consequently, they did not ridicule him as others did. When sober, he did excellent work. His wife died, and so did both his sons. The war claimed one, and the other died in a boating accident. So, Port Charlotte had been unkind to him, so he just gave up.

So, she took the information to the DA. It was like a confession. He was sleeping by the dumpster at Hulle's Grill when the four rapists went into a discussion of the events of the rape. They gloried in what they had done. The chief's son said he drove her hard for that fingernail rake down his cheek, and thinking about it made him excited. He laughed as he urged his friends to look at the evidence.

"Wish I could've stayed longer," the bank manager's son said. "She was warm and giving—I could feel her enjoying it. Tell you, man, them women protest but they don't mean it. Once they experience my fellow, they surrender. Rape my foot. She loved it and wanted more."

"No, fool. Maryanne wanted me. I can deliver the job better than you chumps. I have a lethal but loving weapon."

Shocked at what he heard, he made a sound. The boys heard and started to search so he held his bottle and opened his pants. When they found him—he was the town's drunken sot, asleep with his bottle—they shouted, and he didn't respond. They kicked him, and he grunted. He opened his eyes and then closed them and pretended to doze off. The chief's boy yanked at his bottle and he protested.

"Oh, Doris, my love! I love you more each day." He patted the bottle affectionately. He prayed they believed he heard nothing and understood even less. He fell back, cradling his beloved. The boys then went their way. Even in his foggy mind he could not conceive of what he'd overheard or what they were bragging about. A shiver went through him at the horror and cruelty the boys were bragging about. He had to report it, but who would believe a sot like him. Although he had gone a whole week without a drink prior to this, he would have to sober up, but not too quickly, in case the boys became suspicious. And that's how he confided in Beatrice and swore her to secrecy.

Beatrice could no more keep that knowledge to herself any more than Jesus wouldn't go to the cross. She told Greg that the information was too vital to be withheld. Her empathy was with Maryanne's pain. She remembered when Maryanne wore pigtails—sweet kid. She instinctively knew Clarice needed an ally since the upper crust in the church sided with the alleged perpetrators' mothers. So, she told Clarice, who went to the DA. Greg remained reasonably sober and spoke with DA Ronald McNabb. And the DA had his star witness.

Clarice sighed. Life is not fair. She was so glad back then, but now the criminals were let free and her baby was even more devastated than before. She could not comfort her. *Words are inadequate*, she thought. She had to be strong for Maryanne. She just had to. She could not fall apart. Tears burned the back of her eyes. She blinked rapidly to stem the tears. She felt impotent. She could do nothing. How could she turn the other cheek? Worst, how did they find out about Greg. He was hidden. He ended up in the hospital, hit-and-run accident. Someone found out, and Judge Hornbell could've allowed the videotape the DA made of Greg's statement and interview. Not siding with the defense, he would not be able to cross-examine Greg. The recording made by Rutherford was suppressed—obtained under duress. The judge emasculated the whole case.

Clarice knew the good old boys' network was alive and well. They frequented the same club, drank highballs, cognac, and whatever the hell they drank. In her heart, she couldn't believe that the Chief of Police, Congressman, and banker did not bring pressure on the judge. So she was more than despondent when the judge rejected the DA's request to use the deposition given earlier. The judge in any case has autonomy when it came to the rules of evidence. He could've adjourned the case and reviewed if there was precedence to admit the video evidence. Her research showed Rule 30 (b) 6 on Admissibility: That the witness was unavailable due to illness, hospitalization, and the witness' testimony was based on personal information or just the fact that the information was given to the DA himself. She wondered if she was stretching the rules. But she was convinced an allowance could've been made and would've been if the above group was not involved.

Clarice didn't know why she was so bitterly angry about the verdict. Most of the corroborating evidence that was needed went up the chimney. But she hoped. Did she hope! She believed decency, the truth, the ER doctor's testimony, Rutherford's testimony, the identification of the voice and the ring by both Rutherford and Maryanne, and Maryanne's testimony, and the empathy for Maryanne would help. It did not sway the jurors. And the accused—not testifying by invoking the California Evidence Code 930, the equivalent to the Fifth Amendment—had a privilege not to testify that apparently helped. She remembered everything that went against them: no DNA and, worst of all, the hit-and-run that put Greg in a coma the day before the trial. She was filled with malice and hatred. Poor Maryanne! She knew she was at breaking point. She needed to vent, yet had to be strong for Maryanne. Eyes brimming over, she went over the trial again.

True to her word, Renee got Bridgette, Chad's girlfriend, to retract her earlier alibi. Bridgette was dumb, but her father was manager of Palace Gardens, and her mother ran the local PTA and the local charities or so it seemed. Bridgette was a pretty but dumb girl who put the dumb in the term dumb blonde. Renee hoped she would not forget the crash course she got from her about prison life. Renee told her to withdraw her alibi or she would go to jail for perjury, for lying to the cops. She explained she was covering up the rape of Maryanne by saying Chad was with her. When Bridgette looked wide-eyed, she drove home the point that she would get five years in prison and a fine of over $5,000. She told her that was the good part. When Bridgette asked what she meant, she told her she would suffer the same fate as Maryanne from prison guards, and it would be a revolving door of prison guards on all shifts. After they finish with her, they'd pass her to a queen—a six-feet woman most likely named Helga, and she would be Helga's wife. Renee watched Bridgette's face turn from white to red and every shade in between.

"Now, is that worth it, Bridgette? Will the girls you were with back you up. Do you think they will thank you for drawing them into this horror? Well, what do you say?"

Bridgette spluttered that she gave the alibi because Chad told her he was drinking and if the coach found out he'd be benched or dropped from the team. She knew nothing about any rape. She looked ready to faint, and Renee held her and put her to sit. Holding the back of her neck, she said she would retract her statement to the police; Chad was not with her between 4:30 and 5:30 p.m. Renee told her she was just looking out for her, not wanting her to suffer as Maryanne did. She was glad she didn't have to twist her arm more than she did, but, for security, told her to ask her mother about the punishment for perjury and life in the prison system. She was happy to help her friend Maryanne. Renee also organized the girls to boycott any and all sporting activities. Date rape was a problem in that school which was covered up, and this unprovoked horrific attack against Maryanne was a hundred-time worst and is the illegitimate child of these hushed rapes. So, they protested at the games, much to the chagrin of the school administration. They sported "raccoon" eyes in solidarity with Maryanne. They were shut down in May, and many girls agreed that they would go solo to prom. They did not want dates.

Maryanne crawled back to her bed. Now more than ever she was glad she had addressed the court when the jurors went to deliberate. It was unorthodox they said, but with the DA and his second chair's petition, the judge agreed so she could address the court. It was like a premonition.

"On February 21, I was raped. I am told I am not on trial, but it doesn't feel like it. I've had to listen to the defense attorney, Mr. Mudd, denigrate my character and sling dirt at my name in an effort to free four boys, not one, but four, who raped me. I need to say no one saw anything or heard anything yet, but everyone knows what happened. Oh, it's just talk and would not come forward with what they overheard the defendants say; except one, and he was run down in a hit-and-run accident the day he was sober and to testify for the prosecution. Hear this: Fact 1 I was raped; 2 I do not have or ever had a penis; 3 I did not break the orbit of my eye—a rapist's fist did that; 4 the medical report written and with pictures shouts rape. The DNA material sent to the crime lab along with the specimen from the rape kit would identify the person I scratched in the face that day and would name my rapist, but everything disappeared. Think about the corrupt chief who doesn't have the decency to recuse himself from the case where his son is accused because pops will fix it. Yes, Chad Broome raped me. I scratched his face, and I heard him say the bitch scratched me. And to the parents, upright citizens and pillars of the town who provided your rapist sons with alibis, you are just like them; a chip off the old block. Rapists, all of you. But life is a cycle, remember."

As the judge reprimanded her for her speech, she addressed him.

"And you, Your Honor, never stopped Mr. Mudd from making vile insinuations against me. And you didn't stop him from defaming me about my intentions that day. How can you judge me on my intentions? Where is the reprimand for the destroying of evidence? Yes, and DNA from under my fingernail and the semen. Why not tell your buddy Broome he should not be a part of the investigation? Oh, you are all friends—why did you not recuse yourself? You could have allowed the deposition of Greg Raymond because you know his accident was no accident. The only person in this town with a conscience; the one human who would testify on my behalf involved in a hit-and-run a day before he is to testify. What a coincidence, eh, Your Honor? Poor Greg. He's in a coma. That sit well with you, Judge?"

Judge Humbell turned beet red, and as dissent arose in the courtroom, he banged his gavel. "Order in the court." He had to break for fifteen minutes.

Chapter 5

She came back to the present. Maryanne knew she would leave Port Charlotte. She was not in any condition to go to college—she lacked concentration, focus, was depressed and bitter. She would recuperate for a year and then go on to college. She was broken. She reached out to Denise Sillas to find a psychiatrist or psych nurse practitioner. The help she'd received from Denise seemed to have evaporated. The not-guilty verdict kept knocking at her brain. She slept badly, and when she did, it was from exhaustion. She was very tired and irritated and had very little appetite. She became dependent on yogurt, and it fast became her favorite meal. Her parents tried to whet her appetite, but nothing worked. She went three days per week to therapy (Dr. Yvonne Sheere). Her brain was on fire, and though she tried, she couldn't answer why.

She realized that she had to accept that there was evil; that mankind was evil; that mankind had a choice, and when he chose to be reprehensible, his target could be anyone. Bitter though she was, she didn't want rape visited on anyone. She continued to feel dirty and unclean even though she was going to therapy. There was one day the whole family went except her father. She did not blame him. He had a child bride plus working otherwise amounted to two full-time jobs. *Serve him right*, she thought spitefully. She'd lost everything that mattered: her self-respect, her innocence, the boy she loved, her perspective of the world around her. She mistrusted everyone. She especially didn't want to see or speak with any of the jurors. Those mealy mouth Christians and upright citizens!

One day her mom told her that some television station wanted to interview her regarding the ordeal and the acquittal of the infamous four.

She declined, but they persisted. Later she told them okay. Later the station said she could not name names for possibly libel. She asked what the point would be then. She told them to take a hike, not to call back; she did not want to be harassed. About a month later, WSBN called. She told them that she was not interested. They persisted, and one day they called when Renee was visiting. Renee spoke with them, then told her she got a sweet deal and that she would be able to tell her side of what happened and the results. Renee did not explain how she got them to agree. They would do the interview in a week. Clarice was on board with it. Maryanne asked Clarice and Renee if they thought there could be backlash to her going on television. Both were enthusiastic, and Maryanne rationalized there couldn't be any greater harm than that which was already done, especially since she was telling her truth.

She thought she'd spit out the anger that turned to bile inside. It backed up in her brain, mind, chest, and heart. Maybe she could expel some of the venom she was feeling. She was highly motivated to do nothing and was lavish with her depression until now. She could use some choice words for the Port Charlotte Four. Maryanne began to warm up to the idea and was persuaded to let Renee wash her hair and curl it so it cascaded down her back. However, she still sported the droopy eyelid. So, they got a pair of dark glasses but later changed her mind for a pair of reading glasses just for disguise. Rutherford would not be there. Since their relationship was nonexistent now, she didn't want him there. She didn't hate him or blame him; she just felt naked each time she saw him. She tried to explain to him that she needed time to heal. The irony was that she loved him still. She agreed he could call occasionally, like once per month, not more often. He pleaded, but she didn't change her mind. Maybe one day, but not now. Reluctantly, he accepted it.

The interview was conducted on Thursday, July 16. The family was there, including Renee and Yolande. Her mom would be on camera with her, but not Felix. He was too shy but agreed to be in a family picture at the end if father Gavin showed up. It was a hot July day. The weather seemed cooperative—no rain and a breeze. Ms. Dee Parchment, a reporter, and one cameraman showed up at 11:00 o'clock. Though live, it would be aired Sunday at 6:30 p.m. They brought additional lights, and with the lights in the living room and from the camera, they seemed adequate. They discussed what she'll say before the recording started. She had the questions so she could rehearse privately so she could appear poised and answers seem spontaneous rather than being rehearsed. Maryanne explained about her eye and the reading glasses to disguise the droopy lid.

The interview went very well. She was nervous but was clear and articulate. Her message was straight: wrongdoers must be punished, and social privilege was not a reason to swap decency and honesty. Rape is a crime. She did not rape herself, and she was not going to be sniveling and shrinking anymore. She did nothing to be ashamed of; that there'd be a day of reckoning for those who tamper with Justice whether they are the offspring of the chief of police, the congressman, the banker, or the largest car dealership. He who hides the wrong he does will do it again. To the bought jurors, thieving policemen, and clerks that destroyed evidence and attempted to kill Greg Raymond, a witness, beware of reciprocity. Something was rotten in Port Charlotte! It was reeking. When she was asked why she was being so open, if she wasn't afraid of those who subvert justice, she said no.

They could sue her, but she had zip, and the townspeople made sure she was stripped naked so danger meant nothing to her. She removed her glasses to show her eyes, contrasting with the pictures in the living room. When asked what she wants known, she said, "Evil is an exacting master, and it will revisit the sons, daughters, and grandchildren. My tears will never be in vain, so to the alibi mothers, you will cry too."

They took a family picture with her father barely making it. Renee and Yolande were featured in the last shot. Her mother expressed outrage at the verdict and the leniency granted the criminals versus her daughter.

"That evidence was withheld that would convict Broome, Busch, Spoolson, and Caldern. It is public record that they were booked and tried for rape, and I will always say it. There was a farce of a trial, a mockery to trials everywhere. It was recorded. It's just that there is a two-tier justice system: one for the rich and one for the poor. How could evidence just disappear? And the judge doesn't query it. Doesn't ask for an investigation! There is corruption in high places. So unfair!" Her eyes filled up, and she stopped talking.

There was a turning point from that day. She contacted RAINN (Rape Abuse Incest National Network) and asked about surgery to be done on her eye to correct the saggy eyelid. She still had a way to go and continued her therapy sessions because she still refused to take Valium or even Unisom. Despite her bravado, she was still hurting but refused to give the inhabitants of Port Charlotte the power to hold her hostage. After her surgery, she would leave and start college. She crafted an exercise routine to get her body toned. She was by no means fat but decided she needed to tone her muscles. Maybe if she had. Maryanne halted her thoughts. Four against one was an unfavorable odd. Her physical strength or lack of it had nothing to do with her getting raped. Self-blame was an addiction she was learning through therapy that came quickly, engulfed her being, developed and became riddled with a turtle mentality. As a general rule, she did not hate the turtle, but in this instance she disliked it. But there was always a lesson. The turtle was a survivor, just slow. Patience was not a frock she carried in her closet, even if she could benefit from it.

Wow! She's waxing poetic. She smiled at herself, something she hadn't done in a while. Imagine she and poetry! They did not mix, but it's a thought. Why not try her hand at poetry? What would it hurt? It might prove interesting. She could perhaps expel the demons that haunt her mind; even evict the erstwhile thoughts of blame and self-recrimination. Her therapist was right; it was going to take time and patience—that she had to forgive herself. It made little sense then, but now it did. She blamed herself for the rape—mad that she did not prevent it, that she allowed it to happen. It was almost August, and she needed some peace. Her interview with WSBN would now air August 10th instead on *What's Your Thoughts*, a news magazine. Dee Parchment had assured her it would not be a watered-down version of the actual interview, "their program is new, cutting-edge journalism." They bragged their stories were edgy, unique, and thought-provoking—getting the story behind the story.

Maryanne wondered if her statements would help anyone or just her bitterness spilling over. She hoped people would take a long, hard look at justice, or rather injustice, and that in time it would stop harnessing the true victims with guilt, shame, and denigration. Was our society just a bunch of cowards, turning aside from these atrocities? They certainly were not their brothers' keepers. She reasoned that there were more priests and Levites than Samaritans. Sad but true! Her rape was not their business. Justice for her and Rutherford was not their business. All those jurors and the judge made her look with fresh eyes. It made her understand that it is more important to belong. Yes, "if you let him go, you are not a friend of Caesar."

She wondered at the biblical imagery; Pilate-Judge Humbell. They are both "just" men—Pilate washed his hands publicly but not his heart. Humbell presided over the trial but refused to acknowledge the Federal rule of Evidence, (after he knew all, all-forensic evidence disappeared) and yet Greg's deposition or testimony was denied, claiming the accused had the right to face his accuser. Bile rose in her so strongly she couldn't breathe.

"Mom."

Clarice ran to her and held her. She noticed she was trembling, breathing hard, and her face suffused with color. Clarice held her intoning, "Breathe! Deep breaths!" while doing it herself.

"What's the matter, baby?" she asked brows knit. She lowered her to the seat then got her a glass of water. "What is it, honey? What got you in this state—your breathing is shallow, face red, and pulse throbbing at your neck. You look like you would burst a vessel."

Maryanne's breathing eased, and she drank some of the water. She didn't answer her mother right away, but after taking a deep cleansing breath, she told her it was the acquittal of those barbaric men that just made her incensed; her rational sense left her. She was consumed with rage and bitterness. Deep in her heart she wanted to respond to popping a vessel; would it be that bad. Although she didn't orchestrate it, it would have been a relief. She had these bouts of anger and hate and not as frequently as before. Clarice hugged Maryanne. As long as her daughter suffered, she would too. Her resentment fought to explode as Maryanne's, but she spoke soothingly to her, agreeing it was not fair and should never happen again. She was sorry, but only time would dull the pain and anger, and must find an outlet before it destroyed her completely. She could not be blamed for the evil of the Chelseatta High School Four.

Her mother rocked her, continuing that they had to find a way to deal with it. She asked how the therapy was going, if there was real progress taking place. Maryanne assured her that it helped, although at times, like now, it overwhelmed her; thankfully this severe was not the norm. They sat quietly for a while until Clarice got up. She felt like screaming. The rage inside was tearing her up. She realized hot, burning anger and the futility of wishful thinking. She could not erase her daughter's pain. And there was nothing she could do. She wanted revenge. She was incensed. There was no turning the other cheek. Forgiveness was a commodity in short supply.

Clarice was not a drinker, but she needed a strong drink. She had to kill the pain. She needed to get away, but how? Because of the state Maryanne was in. But she was drowning in impotence. She could do nothing. She found a bottle of whiskey from when Gavin lived there. She poured a glass. That thing was nasty. How did men drink that! It burned her throat going down. She started to cough. Yet, it was a small price to pay. She did not protect her daughter and couldn't even provide her with justice. Clarice ran for some water to neutralize the whiskey. Funny, she thought in a distracted way; she liked wine and champagne, but whiskey was a different animal. Well, the burning in her throat was a perfect match for the burning in her heart. The liquor did the trick. Gradually she calmed down and knew tomorrow she would go to confession.

She had a fitful night. She left her bedroom door open in case Maryanne needed her. She left Maryanne in bed but awake with the assurance that she was okay. Clarice was worried, though. Once at work, she called Renee and asked her to go by later so Maryanne would not be alone. Clarice worked with efficiency to complete her tasks that morning. By mid-morning, she had typed all the cards for the new books. She replaced several other cards, wondering how anyone would get ink and food stains on them. Some were worn, agreed, and needed replacing, but the gooey stuff and chewing gum? She was constantly learning that the human mind and behavior were baffling. At five of twelve, she grabbed her pocketbook and headed for the church.

Traffic was not heavy and reached St. Agnes the Divine quickly. She made the sign of the cross and headed for the confessional. She hoped the priest was there. She saw no one as she hurried forward. She reached the confessional, and she knew Father Leonard Festes was there. She unburdened her soul, the pain she was in and the feeling of hatred for the boys that raped her daughter, her desire to seek revenge, of maiming them and to let them pay. By this she was sobbing. She spoke of the unwillingness of people to testify to what they knew about the rape and the taking of sides by the parishioners. She felt disconnected from the church, which had been such a solace to her. Though Father Leonard tried to pacify, it sounded like platitudes to her. Why she wanted to know why people were so indifferent and didn't want to get involved. Father explained they were people first, to remember the parable of the Good Samaritan. "Sometimes we do not see other people's pain and suffering. Hate is a barren emotion and takes a lot of energy. We fail many times to be our brothers' keeper, and that is why Christ had to die for our sins. Indifference to our brothers' plight is all too common, but we must forgive."

It struck Clarice then—indifference to another's plight. *Oh Jesus*, she thought. "What have I done, what have I done." She didn't realize she'd spoken out aloud.

The Father said, "Peace, my child. You seem agitated. What is it. What have you done?"

Clarice began her narrative. "Back in Mobile, Alabama, there was a young girl, Faith, seven or eight years old, who was attacked. She didn't die but left her traumatized and terrified to go outside. An African American male was charged in the attack, and although he was innocent, he was jailed for this."

"How do you know he was innocent?"

She began to cry louder. "At the time of the attack, I saw the Sawyers brothers talking to the little girl. Charlie (that's the African American's name) was nowhere near there. I told my parents but they said to leave those colored folks' business; if he was innocent, they'd find out in court. She wanted to go tell the police, but her father told her they're not like us. Let them deal with their own problems. I asked what if they didn't find out, but he, my father, insisted I stay out of it. It bothered me for a long time, especially after they burned his house and his dog. His mother barely escaped with her life. Charlie was convicted and sent to jail. I left after they said he was appealing the conviction."

"Are you sure of your facts, child? We cannot blame ourselves for others' misdeeds. However, we can pray and must pray for forgiveness. That is why forgiveness is so important. You must forgive yourself also," said Father Leonard.

Clarice was not that easily consoled. Was this the proverbial "chickens coming home to roost"?

Just as I turned my back on Charlie by not going to the police, so now the same with the rape. I know now it's revisited on my Maryanne. I wish if it had to happen, it would happen to me. My indifference has caught up with me. That's why despite what everyone knew, no one would talk to the police.

Nothing Father Leonard said made her feel better. She was drained emotionally and psychologically. This was payback for Charlie. This was life going full circle. And Maryanne was the lamb.

Clarice got back fifteen minutes late. She moved and worked by rote. Frankly her actions mimicked a zombie. At home she tried to shake her apathy. She desperately wanted to curl into a ball and bawl. When Maryanne commented that she looked tired and maybe she should have an early night, she protested. When Maryanne insisted, she admitted it had been an exhausting day. Clarice was not sure she could face the world tomorrow. She did not want to go to work. After her confrontation with her buried memories, she did not want to exchange polite conversation with coworkers or deal with the public. Where did this memory come from? And why now. How could she work? The public deserved someone who was present with a pleasing demeanor. What would happen from now on? How would she cope? The defunct memories were awake. Conscience rose from the ashes.

With her mind in turmoil, Clarice undressed in the dark. She was distraught. What a cruel hand fate had dealt her. She couldn't quiet her conscience. Not ten minutes after she had seen the Sawyers brothers talking with Faithie, they found her bleeding by the roadside. Ma Blues Eatery was at least two or three miles from there. She was sure other people would've seen them too. What happened to them? And why was Faithie alone, even though she was a stone's throw from where she lived? That did not matter. Her actions were in question. She cringed. She wondered how she had put it out of her mind so completely. If this wasn't karma, what else?

Clarice slept fitfully, and the next morning she called in sick. Her voice was flat and dull, mirroring what she looked like. She used cold water to wash her face to bring color to it. Even with the lights her complexion looked blanched. She had to get some color in her cheeks, or people might think she was the living dead. If it were Halloween, she would not need a costume; it would be "come as you are"—not that she believed in or supported Halloween. She decided to do some stretches to see if the exertion would do her well. It did but under her eyes were baggy and black and blue. For the first time she felt her forty-one years and looked sixty. She needed some distraction. Mid-morning, the phone rang. It was Joan; she wanted to know if she would go to lunch with her and Beatrice. She called the job, and they said she was out. They figured she needed cheering up. She knew they were jovial women, and they laughed a lot. They always seemed so upbeat!

Bea and Joan picked her up. They asked if Maryanne was coming, but she'd declined. They were driving to Punta Gorda. They would go and sit in the park. It was quiet, peaceful and the tall trees were restful. It was a quaint little place. They had a picnic basket—cold cuts, chicken, coleslaw, mac and cheese, cheese, pink lemonade, and apple cider. They had disposable utensils and ice as well.

"Oh, honey!" Bea said. "You need some color in those cheeks and laughter in those eyes. I know it has been rough.

But God is still God and merciful, and we will rejoice. That's what my Mama said."

They sang spirituals and choruses. Clarice was caught up in their singing and was especially moved by "Sing Till the Power of the Lord Come Down." Bea sang lead and Joan sang backup. She began to feel better. Bea opened a red and white plaid tablecloth and took out chicken wrapped in foil from a Pyrex dish, mac and cheese, and cold cuts arranged on a makeshift platter. The food smelled good, and Clarice was looking forward to it. She knew Bea made the best fried chicken (now she knew it was oven-fried). They blessed the food and then began to eat. The chicken and the mac were still warm, and Clarice enjoyed them. She complimented them on the meal. The turkey, ham, and salami were store-bought, as was the cider. Everything else was homemade.

They talked about the library and the children's hour for the summer. Clarice said it was going very well and that the turnout was very good. The ladies talked about the happenings at the Cultural Center. They both enjoyed the drama and the poetry reading. They loved ballroom dancing and the dances they had there. The theater put on plays, and occasionally an out of towner dropped in. There was an ensemble that graced the stage from time to time. Bea encouraged her to come to the end of Summer Gala Labor Day.

Clarice enjoyed their light-hearted talk. They seemed to have no cares in the world. She didn't know how they stayed so upbeat all the time. Joan asked her what was happening with her, how she was doing as well as Maryanne. She said she was doing fine, but Joan wagged her finger:

"It is not fine, Clarice. Those blue-black circles spell stress, fatigue, sadness, and borderline depression, sleeplessness, the works. I'm a graduate from the FSU School of Social Work. I know the signs. Are you seeing someone? Listen, honey, do what you have to do to live, not just survive. Scream if you want to, roar even. See, you are experiencing the blues. Yes, when the world seems upside down, when pain is all you see, feel, and hear, when the world seems right but everything is wrong. When you find out that God's perfect world is not perfect, contaminated by man with drugs, malice, depravity, where the just finds no justice. We know. We were raised by it. We feel your pain. That's why the great Dr. Martin Luther King said, 'Injustice anywhere is a threat to justice everywhere.'

"That's right, sugar. We are intertwined, and what affects you affects me. There's an old adage: Today for me, tomorrow for you. We have to speak up; be our brothers' keepers. When things aren't right, we've got to say so."

Clarice was mortified and could only nod.

Beatrice said, "I will tell you a story. My grandparents are from Mobile, Alabama, but my mother hightailed it out of there at seventeen. So, I didn't grow up there, but we have aunts, uncles there and cousins. My grandparents died, so we didn't see much of the remaining great-aunts and uncles. But Great Aunt Sarah still lived there. In her younger days, she did housework, washed, and ironed. She worked very hard. Her husband died and left her with three sons. One died in an accident, and two enlisted in the army. One died in Vietnam, and Charlie came home. He was a good man, very good at making and repairing things. He lived with Aunt Sarah, his mother. As Aunt Sarah told it, that war messed Charlie up; he wasn't the same, yet he was gentle. He did odd jobs. He'd repair a gate, a chicken coop, a door. He could solder metals, and he loved whittling. He fancied himself a magician and always did magic tricks."

Beatrice paused, lost in remembrance of Charlie's wide eyes and soft smile.

"Everyone knew Charlie, and he moved among the Spanish, Asians, Indians, and whites. Charlie could fix anything. He got a little something from the VA, but he wasn't idle, so he worked so that Aunt Sarah didn't have to. One day, a little white girl, Faith Sanderson, was attacked near her home. Now Charlie knew Faith; he had done work for her father before. Although Charlie was miles away from where

Faithie was hurt, they pinned it on Charlie. The man Charlie was working for wouldn't even corroborate that Charlie was there until reminded he fixed the back gate with him and had unpacked the shed. Only then did he admit Charlie was there but he 'did not know what time he left.' His wife was prevailed upon to verify that Charlie was there. She testified she was doing her 'Christian duty by telling the court Charlie was there. She doesn't rightly know what time he left but reckon it was about two or two thirty.' Charlie was eating apple pie at Ma Blues Eatery at 2:45 p.m. but managed to attack Faithie at 3:15 p.m. The attack took place two miles from there. The waiter and other patrons testified he was there in the eatery up to 3:00 p.m. He could not cover two miles in less than fifteen minutes on foot. Mobile, Alabama was determined to hold Charlie accountable. He was arrested, allegedly tried, and found guilty and sentenced to twenty-five years, five years more than the Caucasian man who killed his girlfriend. They had tons of evidence against him. He only got twenty years' imprisonment. Yes, Faithie was badly hurt, and she was so little, poor mite, but she did not die. And five witnesses—even Mrs. Stewart, doing her Christian duty, though wouldn't confirm the time—testified on Charlie's behalf but did not save him. They burned his mama's house and his dog. Aunt Sarah barely escaped with her life. No one saw anything. Just as your case—nobody saw the arsonist.

"Given the climate and hostility of Mobile, they deliberately put this older man, a veteran, in general population, put out the word that the n**** attacked a white child. He was beaten, blinded in the left eye by one of the white inmates. His leg was broken, and due to lack of medical attention thereafter, walked with a limp. He said he realized he was safer in Vietnam than in Mobile. He was despised because of his dark skin, and he was never in doubt that it was so. 'You got off light, n—We intended to finish you off, but you are a tough bastard.' Based on that, he was moved to solitary confinement. All during that time Aunt Sarah visited him, carrying him his favorite pecan pie. They permitted it after she cried, telling them he was a US vet and how he went to Vietnam. Charlie was locked up for ten years until he was exonerated. Appeal after appeal was turned down until finally the NAACP sent a good lawyer and the public defender dismissed.

"Faith was a feeble child after the attack. She contracted bacterial meningitis and died two years later. After the attack, she stayed home and was homeschooled. She had a nurse, Doris (really a helper), an African American woman who took excellent care of her. After Faith died, the mother kept the room as a shrine. Everything remained the same. Five years after Faith's death, Mrs. Sanderson called Doris and told her to take the clothes and the books. Doris did, and she came across a notebook, and in it was a letter to Jesus. The gist of the letter is that John and Eli Sawyers hurt her. They told her they would teach her a trick. They hit her with a piece of board. She wanted Jesus to forgive her and them. She said Charlie was her friend.

"So, a voice from the grave exonerated Charlie, but jail had broken him. He always believed he would be found innocent. The voice of one white girl did what five eyewitnesses of color who provided airtight alibis could not do. The thirteen- and twelve-year-old boys confessed. They were seventeen and eighteen by then. And the wonderful Mayor said it was an honest mistake that was made. For the first time, I looked at hate. I realized they were barren people, devoid of conscience, hate mongers, most despicable people and knew I should not breathe the same air as them. Without a doubt, it was his skin color that was on trial and got convicted. Believe Dr. King alluded to that."

Beatrice stopped her monologue and gasped. Clarice was as white as a sheet and trembling. She seemed to be gasping for air. "What is the matter?" Joan started to fan Clarice while telling her to breathe easy. Gradually her breathing returned. The pallor of her skin was heightened by the strawberry lipstick she had put on that morning. What a cruel fate that the two women who befriended and supported her before and throughout the trial turned out that Charlie was their relative. It didn't matter that Joan was not related to Charlie as she was close to Beatrice like sisters. She was devoid of emotion. Bea asked if Charlie's story upset her, and she nodded in sympathy.

"If you are that upset, imagine Great Aunt Sarah. She got her opportunity to tell them the day Charlie was released. There was a reporter there and asked her how she felt. Fifty years of bottling up came out. And she said this:

'My Charlie is a decent man. Served his country though it hates and spurns him. No one can be in two places at once. Five African American witnesses testified he was at Beas but the prosecutor and the judge proceeded anyway, and twelve *honest* jurors listened and found him guilty. Yet no one saw him hit this baby or anything. If a white boy or man had such an alibi and five witnesses, he would've been acquitted. But twelve biased people, ninnies, were there and a jackass for a DA and a buzzard for a judge found nothing wrong convicting an innocent man. No evidence against Charlie except a super selected jury. But I do not know why I expect honesty and decency from people who enslave others, rob them, and worst, rape their mothers. You raped Africa because that is the Motherland. You desecrate the people and the land, stealing their artifacts and imprisoning their sons and daughters, making them work for free building this country so you bastards can amass wealth. Yes, you make the Negro's color a weapon against him so you can denigrate him. But listen well, it does not take integrity to pillage and murder.

Doesn't take any character to be a thief. Just how you think of us, we think even less of you. You are thieves and murderers everywhere you go. And for good measure, rape the natives here too. You continue your despicable ways by killing the indigenous people, taking their land and rounding them up like cattle, and putting them in pens called reservations. Reservation! Their own land. All over the world you take, you menace. You are the boss. Who the hell bequeathed Africa and America to Europeans? Although I believe it is the dregs that settled here. How is it that you came here on the Mayflower and the other people are migrants? That does not make you indigenous. I hope you all rot while still alive and the maggots are your comfort. Have the guts to print it, you contemptible curs. Your day is coming. She turned, spat at the feet of the Mayor, tossed her head, and walked off head high. And they made a path for her. In all the years I've known Aunt Sarah, I never knew she was that eloquent. But as a mother defending her child, she was fierce. She never stopped believing in Charlie's innocence—Charlie was fine until he went to war, and upon his return, he became child-like. Look how they reward him.'"

By this time Clarice was white as Macy's bright and white sale. Joan searched her bag for smelling salts and gently waved it under Clarice's nose, assuring her the story was not intended to upset her but to commiserate with her. They implored her not to internalize all that. That if more people would empathize and be as disgusted as she was with injustice and hate, maybe things would not be as bad or hurtful; that honesty and neighborliness should be ideals society lives up to.

The ladies apologized for going down memory lane, which resulted in causing her distress when the point of the lunch was to cheer her up. They asked for forgiveness. Clarice was aghast. "Oh Lord Jesus," she whispered inwardly, "help me."

The ladies broke into songs to cheer her up, singing "I'm Going to Lay Down My Burden Down by the Riverside." Meanwhile they sang; she prayed and tried to steady her breathing and shut off thoughts of Charlie.

How cruel that Bea, who reached out to her, was a friend to her, was related to Charlie. Fate is an ancient ancestor that calls us to account, she thought. Someone is having a good laugh at her expense. She even feels worse than when she spoke with Father Leonard; she did not know she would be confronted with this. The chickens did come home to roost, and all the "Kum Ba Yah," "Hear O Lord the Sound of My Call" soothed little.

That night Clarice slept in bits and pieces. Charlie's smooth, placid, chocolate face invaded her sleep. Charlie, with the gentle smile, blind in one eye, and walks with a limp. She woke up bathed in sweat. Guilt gnawed at her conscience. How could she accept Beatrice's friendship now? She felt like Arthur Dimmesdale in *The Scarlet Letter*. She could not rationalize her actions regarding Charlie. At age eighteen or nineteen, she knew right from wrong. She liked Charlie, and her conscience replied, but not enough to speak on his behalf. Her parents insisted it would right itself and it was the colored people's business. If he were innocent, he would go free. But why can't I tell the cop what I know, she asked. Her father said she knew nothing and to keep out of it. And he added, "What would the neighbors think, getting mixed up with that, insisting the colored were not like them?" She capitulated.

So now the shoe was on the other foot. Justice for Maryanne!

She was in despair. She wondered if feeling contrite is enough. She needs all of Psalm 51, yet fear cemented her feet. She cannot blame her parents for not speaking when she should have. Deep in heart she knew she could've made a difference in the trial. Who was she kidding in Alabama back then! Isn't that the reason she left after the guilty verdict. Her silence held Charlie prisoner. Now she wished she'd had the courage to stand up. She tried to find comfort in Father Leonard's words but could not remember them. It was a long time, but the tentacles of time reached back to thrust indifference and hypocrisy in her face, and had no way to turn. She could not look away. It didn't matter now who she was— Priest or Levite—because a Samaritan she was not.

This time her conscience was not so easy to control. Her heart was battered. She was tossed about. She had been dragged by an emotional fiend and spat out on the shore of guilt, remorse, and condemnation. As she sat there, she sought refuge from her tumultuous thoughts; the words came to her: "The sacrifices of God are a broken spirit; a broken and contrite heart, O God, thou wilt not despise." Clarice went back to confession. Father encouraged her to forgive herself; that if she truly believed that Christ died for all people, no matter what they had done, she could ask forgiveness and receive that pardon. Mankind controlled its own heart and chose its direction. She could not know for sure the gentleman would've been acquitted, but the power of God heals. Meditate on God's words. Read Psalm 51 and 1 Corinthians 13. She had to make peace with herself and then with others.

Chapter 6

The much-anticipated interview by WSBN was aired as promised. There was a nice introduction by Dee Parchment ending with "What are your thoughts?" Renee came by to watch with Maryanne and her mother. Renee was excited to see her friend on TV. She'd helped Maryanne pick the dress she was to wear. Turquoise and white photographed well, and Maryanne looked beautiful. True to Dee Parchment's word, it wasn't too watered down and reflected her feelings and facts. She freely called the perpetrators as she talked about the confession on tape that was inadmissible, the hit-and-run accident of a key witness now in a coma. The conspiracy of the disappearance of forensic evidence and of her being violated by the rapists, then the so-called justice system.

However, she's in therapy, taking a self-defense class, and would attend college next fall.

The airing of the interview created a stir. That evening Rutherford came over unannounced. His high cheekbones, big dreamy light green-blue eyes, strong jawline, and that luxurious black hair were the envy of many women. He complimented her on the interview and her bold, unapologetic stand. He commented on her naming Cal, Matt, Griffen, and Chad. She asked him what he thought they would sue. She had nothing, so they had nothing to get, whereas she could for violating her civil rights. She shrugged.

Rutherford asked her quietly why she hadn't told him of the interview. He would gladly be by her side. He wanted to know why she put distance between them. He loved her, and she was shutting him out. He wanted to know why. He was baffled. She could not begin to explain the denigration she felt. Who would want their boyfriend to see them at their worst? She'd thought they were more than friends, but that was last February 21. He did not witness the rape, but he knew what had happened. Why would he want used goods—how could she live thinking that each time he looked at her, he wasn't remembering her shame. Then he'd start inventing reasons not to be intimate with her.

No, Rutherford as handsome and perfect as you are, I cannot take the chance that you will reject me later. Truth was, she missed him terribly. She had been mourning silently the loss of their relationship.

They looked at each other, deep and long, searching. As the light flickered across her features, she was unbeknownst most alluring in her green and white dress and her tumbled hair framing her face. In that instance, Rutherford had never seen such a vision of beauty. As if mesmerized, he leaned forward and captured her lips in a long, passionate kiss that went on and on. There was tenderness and gentleness and sweetness wrapped in one. She didn't resist, and as his tongue slipped between her lips—she forgot everything. That was not one kiss. It awoke something deep and elemental within her. And desire stirred her breast, and on that tide of emotions felt abandoned when he lifted his head and said: "You are the most beautiful girl in Port Charlotte." He leaned forward again and captured her cherry-red lips, devoid of lipstick. And the desire she felt earlier returned with emphasis. He released her and said, "I leave for FGCU (Florida Gulf Coast University) tomorrow. Wait for me."

He left. Tears rolled down her cheeks, hot and scalding. They were tears for her and for him. They were tears of lost love, of what might have been. Rutherford left for FGCU. When he saw the injustice of the rape, he changed his major from Accounting to Forensic Science. That would be more beneficial for victims like Maryanne. What the police did was paltry by standards. There seemed no passion for justice or the truth. He vowed he'd be the top man in forensics in the US, then he'd try for global. There was a rush in his belly when he thought about it. He was excited about the learning and possibilities of processing and recreating crime scenes. He will be relentless. "I'll get justice for you yet, Maryanne. I know they buried the evidence. They cheated and connived." As his thoughts raced toward Orlando and his future, his heart backtracked to Maryanne looking so beautiful, vulnerable yet innocent. She was quite a beauty, and he wanted to wrap his arms around her, keep her safe, and ease her pain. But she would not let him. She rebuffed him for months. But he smiled contentedly; she had feelings for him—those kisses were worth it. Yes, and fifteen minutes of icy cold shower also!

Clarice had never felt so alone as she did at this time. She went to Dino's Liquor and bought herself a bottle of Beaujolais, a red wine with a fruity taste. The mood she was in, it didn't even matter what it was. She really wanted to get good and drunk, but that was a luxury she could not afford. She sought to draw on inner strength but came up empty. She vaguely remembered Father Leonard's words. Mankind was unpredictable, and no one had control over another's actions except for him. And that was why she felt partly responsible for Charlie being blind in one eye and walking with a limp. His neighbors hated him; they did what the war couldn't do: made him a cripple! This was an expensive lesson for her. Her beautiful and innocent daughter paid the price. If that isn't so, why did she remember at this precise time? Of its own volition, her mind made the comparison. She remembered so clearly the frenzy she was in to get people to go to the police to share what they had heard of the perpetrators. Her state was akin to madness. She was driven.

Truly exhausted, Clarice admitted there's nothing she could do for her daughter now, just love and support her. She had to go on living for both children—Maryanne as well as Felix. Poor Felix, who adored his father, only saw him sometimes, once a month. She admitted she was not in control and decided to give it to God as Father Leonard suggested: to leave it at the cross. However, she decided that as soon as she mustered enough courage, she would tell Beatrice and Joan about Charlie and her silence. She could not continue to accept their friendship without confessing. She had clung to their friendship like a lifeline during Maryanne's ordeal. Their support and open friendship kept her when others in the church avoided her. Now she had them as friends and wanted to keep them. These two did not judge her or Maryanne. With that resolve, all she had to do was do it. She prayed for the courage she needed.

Rutherford came to visit. She did miss him. That kiss was a plus, plus. If he had been kissing her like that before, where would her life be? Would her life be different from now? She realized pride was a cold companion to loneliness. Her pride made her pull away from Rutherford. Now she regretted the pride that prompted that action. *No! No!* Her mind screamed. *Not there. I am not going there.* She determined she was not venturing into regret mode. That was one garden she was not entering. It was a fertile breeding ground for self-pity, despondency, and depression.

She had to fight the maelstrom of emotions clamoring for supremacy.

They must be stopped. She inhaled deeply. *Dear Lord, help me. I am tormented.* She had a thirst and a desperate longing for Rutherford. She realized her mistake. She was losing the one man she could ever love.

Rutherford's leaving galvanized her into action. She would continue with therapy and next year most definitely leave for nursing school, wherever. She had something to prove to her rapists, their families, the judge, police-chief, the banker, the car dealer, and the congressman. She owed them so much. Rutherford leaving was the catalyst that lifted her from her apathy. She was determined to control her life. There were days when she would fall, but she would never yield. Thus, she decided to start by getting a manicure and a pedicure with Renee and Yolande. Both enrolled in the St. Joseph School of Nursing and were scheduled to leave Wednesday so it was a farewell. She loved them. They proved to be friends, and she was grateful. She contacted RAINN, and they paved the way for her to have corrective surgery on her saggy eyelid. Now she had something to look forward to—to go to college, study nursing, but not in Port Charlotte. She would research and see which university offered the best possibilities. She abandoned thoughts of Duke and Kaiser. She would find another where nobody knew her or her situation. She would change the color of her hair; try to regain the weight she'd lost and start going to the gym to build muscle tone, making good on her interview statements. She would seek part-time employment somewhere, maybe in Fort Myers and hope no one recognized her. Yes, being a home health aide three days a week would be ideal. She could save for when she leaves next July for school. She would see her friends for one more summer and maybe Rutherford. Yes, that was doable. For the first time in a long time, she was excited about the future. She would not dwell on what she had lost with Rutherford but rather on the gain.

Chapter 7

With that decision taking root, she contacted WRAINN for her surgery; and now she had focus and a mission. Maryanne could've found training as a home health aide in Port Charlotte but would rather go to Fort Myers. In the meantime, she was working to navigate the federal red tape to get the surgery for her eye. She just wanted the groundwork laid so that when she was ready, it would run smoothly. She was ambivalent about whether to do it now or just prior to departure. She planned to ask the doctor to alter her appearance ever so slightly—not drastic, just enough. She had a mission to return to Port Charlotte. She had to thank the infamous four and their families.

Maryanne did her training successfully and had two cases, two four-hour cases. She would work twenty-four hours three days per week. She liked her cases. Miss Lydia had a stroke and had deficits. She used a walker and lived alone. She lived in a three-bedroom house. It was a beautiful house, or it used to be. There're signs of aging but a little TLC will restore it. She was there to make breakfast and cook dinner and package them in containers to warm in the microwave. She assisted her to shower, but she could dress herself, although at times, her arms got weak and her gait wobbly. She liked Miss Lydia and took pleasure in helping her. She knew it's good practice if she's to do nursing. This practical experience would serve to show if she had the empathy and dedication to serve the infirm and sick community.

Her second case, Mr. Worrell, she labeled grumpy. He was a querulous old man. However, she didn't mind him. He also was a stroke victim. His right side was affected, and he was right-handed. He was opposed to her helping him shower. As a peace offering, she offered to close her eyes when she showered him. As a compromise, he placed a hand towel across his lap while she was washing his back and upper torso. She understood and let him keep his privacy. One day she overheard him saying a little kid was coming to wash him. She also made a deal with him to wash him only twice out of the three days she worked with him. He didn't know her story, and no reason he should have. He didn't know he had nothing that interested her, but she's grateful for his grumpiness. She had heard the horror stories of these dirty old men.

She tried hard to appease him, finding out his favorite foods and buying them. She made quiche in small, individual-type aluminum loaf tins. She found out from his friend Bill that he liked it, so she surprised him one day. For the first time, he smiled. Since then, she had made it bi-weekly. He still used the towel across his lap, but for the smile she called it a victory. Her work was going well, and she finally scheduled the surgery for June the following year. That should give her ample time to get her healed, stowed and packed and away to FSU. She would go early; very few people would see her, plus she would be sporting shades. Anyway, the Florida sun would be very hot. (She learned that Rutherford would be doing an internship in DC. No need to stay). Surprisingly the year passed fairly quickly. She made the necessary preparations for her transition to Tallahassee. It's a little disconcerting; she had been to Orlando and to Disney but never Tallahassee. Well let the adventure begin. She felt secure that she would meet no one there she knew. She was going to live on campus and, just by looking at it, believed she would need a map. She was intimidated by its size. Maybe she should've picked a smaller school with a smaller population, but anonymity was crucial to her survival and success. She would have to be careful in class discussions. Since date rape was bound to come up, she would have to walk on eggshells, as her grandmother used to say. The worst part about her leaving was Felix. She knew he was so lost when their parents divorced. She could not understand her father's insensitivity to Felix. It's like he forgot how Felix idolized him. However, he was surviving. His acne was gone and was only a memory. He still continued to use the acne set from Mary Kay.

The day arrived, and she stowed her suitcase and duffel bag and backpack in her mother's car. She wanted to take the train, but no such luck. She believed it's the best way to travel long distances. Anyway, her mother's car would have to do. She gained all of five pounds and was happy about it. That's a benefit of being an HHA. She had to cook for both clients and invariably ate too. She believed it's good practice. Her friends, Renee and Yolanda, surprised her with gifts she could not look at until she reached college. She could not begin to guess what those two were up to. She's going to miss them fiercely. (They were ahead in their studies, having registered last year and started the nursing program). As she took another look around to make sure she had everything, she sighed. They prayed before they left. Her father said goodbye yesterday, but at the last-minute chased her mother down to hand her snacks and lunch from Publix. They could all smell the fried chicken and imagine rolls and vegetables as well.

The campus was huge and looked as confusing as she feared. She wanted to get back into the car. Fortunately, there were students—Sophomores or Seniors—who were there to offer help and directions through the process. Once she was registered, she was directed to her dorm room. There's an overlap of rooms, and she had no room. She had to sit and wait until this was straightened out. Feeling bewildered and slightly lost, she sat with her hand resting under her chin. It was then she heard a voice.

"Hey girl, you lost? Nobody wants you? Hmm and such a pretty little thing too!"

She looked up at the smiling face of a beautiful girl in green Capri and a yellow blouse.

"A ask a question. You lost? Nobody's child. It's a good thing you see me. I will take you man. You look harmless enough."

Maryanne laughed. She liked this girl. She's open and unpretentious. There's an accent—familiar.

"Sort of. My room is double booked so I'm waiting for them to find me a place to live. That's my mom Clarice and brother Felix, and I'm Maryanne Radieux."

She turned. "Glad to meet the Is. Now, this I am Elizabeth Poplyn. You can use any part of the name or all of it except Liza," she said affably.

Everyone was laughing. Maryanne hoped most, if not all, she met had this open friendliness.

"Elizabeth, are you a Sophomore or Junior?"

"Me, oh no. I'm an incoming freshman they call me. Why?"

"You seem like you have been here before," said Maryanne.

"Well, it's my culcha (culture). A so we nuff!"

"Ah?" said Maryanne. Elizabeth laughed.

"We are versed in making ourselves comfortable wherever we go," said Elizabeth, dropping the pronounced Jamaican accent.

"I'm from the inventor of the No problem man land. Know where that is? Jamaica. Just like to tease you, but hold a minute. My roommate withdrew from the program, so you want to room with me? You look lost. I feel I should take you under my wings."

Maryanne was enthusiastic. "Oh sure! You think they will?"

"Watch me," she said. "Ms. Senior the daughter there needs a place to live. I'm willing to take her in. Can you work it?"

"Oh, I'm not sure. We can't just do that," said the student rep.

"Ah right. Point me to the person in charge. I'll do it myself since you can't help," said Elizabeth.

"Just a minute ah-mm, Ms. Elizabeth," she supplied.

"Let me see how I can be of assistance. What's your name?"

Elizabeth turned and beckoned Maryanne over. After about ten minutes it was resolved and they moved Maryanne's things into the room.

It is quite spacious, Maryanne thought. *Maybe I will like it here. Elizabeth is a great addition.* She fell in love with her roommate. She had questions but it could wait. Elizabeth wasted no time in moving her stuff to accommodate Maryanne. Elizabeth told her to feel free to change anything she liked, but not move the Coat of Arms, Jamaican flag or pictures of the National Heroes from the wall, telling her the heroes would grow on her. Maryanne prayed nothing would change between them. There's a kitchenette, and Maryanne took out her hotplate, and Elizabeth burst out laughing.

"It's okay. Girl after my own heart. You should see what I carried with me. Jerk chicken, bammy escovitch fish, jerk pork, ginger beer, June plum and cherry juice, and tamarind. I will not miss my food for a long time. Thank the Lord for a working freezer." It was Maryanne's time to laugh.

"Did you leave anything home for anyone else? How did you carry all that food?"

"Put it that they stow away. Anyway, it's raw food they are concerned about and most of these are canned and bottled stuff," said Elizabeth.

"Tell me which name you prefer," said Maryanne.

"Oh, make it Liz—easy to remember and hard to forget. So, Felix what grade are you? Play any sports?"

"Twelfth. I play baseball, not good at football, really bad at athletics and basketball is passable," said Felix.

"So, which do you prefer? Identify that one and work at it. Or just enjoy it. Sports keep you trim. Right?" said Elizabeth.

Felix smiled and nodded, "True."

That set the stage for their relationship. Maryanne learned a lot about Jamaican culture: the coat of arms, homage to the indigenous people, the Taino, and more so their motto—Out of Many, One People. It's to unify all inhabitants and acknowledge the different persons who lived there and especially the present residents who live there irrespective of what they look like, talk like, etc. It's a blending and coming together as one people. She learned of Swamp Safari, the Crocodile Haven; Lovers Leap, where two young lovers believed to have jumped to their deaths rather than be separated by their slave master; and the famous Dunn's River Falls. And Milk River Bath, which sprang from inside the rocks that was warm and believed to have healing properties, especially for the joints. Maryanne, listening, longed for the peace and tranquility Liz described. She learned too that Liz had two brothers and two sisters. They had a strong resemblance to each other, but with varying heights and shapes. She had headshots of all of them. They seemed happy. The parents were handsome. That explained the children's looks. They seemed very happy.

As the two friends bonded Maryanne was a little self-conscious that she's not as open as Liz, not that she revealed too much personal stuff.

She spoke more about her family and culture. Maryanne wondered if she was a virgin and what she would think if she knew of her disgrace. She had come to rely on Liz's bubbling personality and how beautiful she was inside and out. She made friends easily unlike her. At times she fretted that she would run into someone who knew her. That made sleeping difficult at times. One day Liz asked her what was wrong because she heard her mumbling in her sleep. She put it down to a nightmare and shrugged. Liz looked at her with raised eyebrows but didn't push it. She knew in her heart Liz would be discreet and not reveal anything if she confessed, but it's a secret she wanted to hide.

About three months after they became roommates, Maryanne had another nightmare. She was thrashing and fighting in her sleep, saying "no, no," and Liz woke her up.

Later in the day Liz jokingly said, "Chile, you behave as if duppy deh pon you. All that fighting you doing in yuh sleep! You must say your Our Father prayer. Home we would sen you to sea to teck a sea bath. Know what, weekend we going. Yuh need to rid yuhself (yourself) of all them duppy."

Maryanne laughed, asking, "What is duppy?

"Ghosts or zombies. In Ja, we call them duppy. Fallen angels or people who die without knowing Christ and not going to heaven. They roam the earth because their souls are in torment. So, Satan have them haunting people," said Liz, laughing. "But seriously you too young to have circles around your eyes. And you have shadows in your eyes. Honey, if it's a man he ain't worth it. It's his loss. You are beautiful, bright, and a blessing to this world. Hear me. God didn't have time to make a nobody," she said, hugging Maryanne.

As they hugged Maryanne said, "You really take in strays. Thank you for an unconditional friendship, caring, and compassion. Thanks for looking out for me."

"No problem, man," said Liz, deeply moved.

Maryanne was the beneficiary of Liz's expertise. Liz was an RN registered in the accelerated Master's program, which made the pairing unusual and unheard of. But whatever fate aligned to bring them together was to her advantage. Liz was very knowledgeable and very bright. She was no slouch herself, so with this additional help, her first semester was much more manageable and less strenuous than anticipated. Plus, Liz was a terrific cook, and she realized she loved all Jamaican food Liz cooked. She's surprised Liz was not married and said so.

"Honey Chile, I am not going to be anybody's housewife only. I'll be his helpmeet to give him a wife or companion. There's a time and a place for everything under the sun, and now is the time for education—a Master's Degree. Then, I'll marry Douglas Zane Machado. But he's a good cook. That's why I love his mother, Sylvia. She taught him to cook. I don't want a man to reach home and wait for me to come home and cook. Never happen! We share and share together," said Liz.

"Really, Liz? I would love to see that," said Maryanne, her laugh echoing in the room.

Liz encouraged her to have her own friends and join study groups. It's important to be a part of the class experience. If they waste time and do not study, she could hang around for a bit then break away. However, not being a part of one may be viewed as being antisocial, and one may become isolated. She heeded the advice and joined a study group. She admitted to the study group that she was shy and didn't go out much; rather, she preferred a good book, listening to music, or doing crossword puzzles. She told them that her favorite author was Robert Ludlum. She told he wrote about spies and corruption in high places mostly, and his books were translated into over thirty different languages.

Maryanne marveled at Liz's wisdom, yet she's barely twenty-one years old. She was positive, well rounded and brilliant. She's on scholarship and was eager to go home to Douglas Zane. She heard her many times talking with Zane. And on occasions laughed out but mostly in soft tones, and telling how she missed him. It's their phone date, she told Maryanne. They talked weekly for an hour. The others were spot checks; she called them. Maryanne couldn't believe the level of sophistication in one so young. However, she seemed unapologetically a hundred percent Jamaican and proud of it.

At the end of their first year, she's acclimatized to the Jamaican culture. Liz invited her home. She's surprised how normal the family was. They took it in stride that Liz brought her friend home. She felt welcomed. Liz wasn't joking when she said they looked alike. The pictures did not do them justice. She loved their energy and passion. Liz and Mike were the mischievous ones, and Raymond was a quiet prankster who adopted Maryanne. The three young ladies plus one were more than a match for the men. Mike's wife also joined the female squad to the dismay of her husband. They woke early and hit the beach in Trelawny and had breakfast there as well. It's an idyllic summer. Her home was forgotten as she played water polo without a net.

They visited Dunn's River Falls—the cascade was amazing. The falls was challenging to climb, but she did it with the aid of Raymond. Later they visited Northern Jerkies for jerk chicken, pork, festival, and fish in any style. She was fast becoming addicted to the coconut water and the jelly. It's pure, clean, and refreshing. She liked Douglas Zane. He's tall, handsome, and totally in love with Liz. He's so easygoing; she couldn't see him as Lieutenant. His eyes followed Liz all around, and he had this smile that said "I know something you don't." The amazing thing they all paid compliments, but none of them hit on her. The strangers did, but not one family member did; even Mike's brothers-in-law were polite.

There's a wealth there she had never seen. Yet, they were not opulent, but she guessed it's the aura they exuded; the polished, refined people who lived comfortably and were comfortable in their own skin. There's the promise of a spectacular sunset in Negril, and she could not wait. They did not exaggerate its beauty. For sure nobody could walk away from a Negril sunset. Nobody was never ever the same. Her throat was dry and her eyes were misty. It's as if you can reach out and touch it. It seemed like the Earth or the Sun was paying obeisance to the God that created them. The colors were an explosion of hues, various shades of gold, bronze, purple, and orange. There were several rings, and she knew someone must've seen a magnificent sunset and invented the kaleidoscope. Her first year after graduation, she would take her mother and Felix to Ja. They needed to see this. Maybe that's the wealth concealed by the Poplyns, the intangibles and the closeness they shared.

After a sumptuous meal of crabs, lobster, and jerk pork, Maryanne could hardly move.

"Oh, my goodness! So much food, so little time. I like the boiled coconut milk with the codfish. Can I have that for breakfast tomorrow?" asked Maryanne.

"Oh yes, honey chile. Know all that is showing behind you. So now you cannot point finger at me anymore," said Liz.

Maryanne was shocked at the weight gained but consoled herself she would only have one more breakfast. Run-down was fast becoming her favorite. But then all Jamaican foods were her favorite. She was acting like a kid—eating everything. She wished she could stay with Liz's family. They were very happy and laughed a lot. Liz's grandfather was eighty years old but could well pass for sixty. He was tall, erect in khaki shorts and T-shirt with salt and pepper hair combed backwards. They provided their own entertainment. Evening was family gathering time. The backyard was big and spacious—a mixture of grass and concrete with a cricket field. This was where family and friends gathered, sitting on the grass, chairs, loungers, and benches. Alongside the house was a long table with miscellaneous things—food, utensils, snacks, and fruits.

Liz revised her opinion—they were comfortable and everyone worked except Deon. She was doing A-Levels and was to follow her brother into pharmacology if she didn't change her mind.

Zane stopped by before going to the barracks. Once he left, Liz sat quietly, her brow furrowing.

"What's the matter?" Maryanne asked.

"We leave in ten days, honey. El Zane just reminded me and wants us to go away. But I remind him that would mean leaving you."

"Oh no, Liz. He's so sweet. He never complains when everyone is together. You deserve some me-time with him, plus I'm family now. I can stay with Mom and Dad and the rest of the family. You are so kind and compassionate taking in a stray like me. Be with him. Please go, or I will feel guilty. Ah right. Man, cool and everything irie."

"The sista can bubble. I and I ah right," said Maryanne, fully Jamaican.

"Okay yaadie. No problem man!" And both began to laugh.

Chapter 8

They returned to Orlando amid hugs, kisses, and tears. They continued to room together. Maryanne was aware Liz had only one semester left as she was on the fast-track Master's Degree—she's also working on being a Nurse Practitioner. The Jamaican was an excellent student despite her casual and jovial personality; she was a shark in the classroom, in the books, and about education. About three weeks after their return, Maryanne's peace was rattled. She talked with her mother, who told her Mrs. Busch, Spoolson, and Broome asked about her and said they hoped she was getting help for her trauma.

"Why did you have to tell me this, Mom? Why are you even talking to them? I left to get away from them, from that town. I had a wonderful time in Jamaica. People saw and loved and embraced me. I was happy for the first time in two years. Why didn't you leave me be? I don't want to hear about them. They ask tell them to kiss my you-know-what. Goodbye, mother."

Liz walked in, but Maryanne was unaware of her presence. She was bawling. Liz hugs her.

"Oh honey. You were shouting. What is wrong?"

"It's nothing," said Maryanne.

"Really? They could hear you all the way in the cafeteria. It's too late. You are family. You are going to share. I want that vivacious, happy person that was in Jamaica. Come!" Liz led her to the sofa, her hand around her shoulders.

"Slow down, honey!" she hugged and kissed her on the forehead.

"Auntie Liz is here. I will protect you from all evil. And if necessary, will get Lt. Zane Machado and the Poplyn massive. Okay. Warm shower and bed. You still look a little shaky. I'm going to make my ten-minute chicken noodle soup and you will feel better," said Liz.

Maryanne hastily went to shower so she could cry. The water would hide her sobs. She wanted to scream. She resented her mother for stealing her euphoria. She cried while the water cascaded over her. She remembered Dunn's River Falls and the cool water caressing her body. She was so happy in Jamaica. She actually forgot the horror of being raped. It must be a conspiracy to keep her unhappy. She let the water run over her to wash away the stain of dread and uselessness. She knew she could not hide forever and slowly dried herself. Liz had a steaming bowl of soup ready. It's much easier to follow Liz's directions, so she got into bed, and Liz carried the soup on a tray and placed it across her lap. Reluctantly she drank and knew if she made a good show of it Liz would be satisfied. After a while it grew on her.

"If you are going to be sad, don't do it on an empty stomach, said Liz. Are you going to be okay?"

Maryanne shrugged. "I know I shouldn't get upset, but I can't help myself. Still think you made the best choice for a roommate?" she said forlornly.

"No. But I made an excellent choice. Wouldn't trade you for the world. Besides, I wouldn't be able to go back home. Grandpa would have to pick me up in secret and hide me. My parents and siblings would disown me," said Liz.

She smiled and Liz handed her Pretty, the teddy bear.

"If there's something I can do to help, let me know. No need to carry a burden when there's no need to. I can sense it goes beyond losing a boyfriend and remember you can get help from a professional. I can be your support, whatever it is. Like I said, we are family. Anything you want, need, I am here. I'll leave you to decide what, if anything, you want to share. And if you need something, just call. Love you, baby," said Liz.

Maryanne wanted to unburden herself to Liz so bad but what could Liz do. Liz was sensitive and would not judge her; she's sure, yet she hesitated. The nightmares had subsided, but despite the number of times she asked "Are you okay?" she never pried. She pushed her with schoolwork but that was it.

Please, Lord, let this go away and let me be at peace.

What was worse, she was missing Rutherford. She'd actually forgotten him in Jamaica, and as soon as she returned, he was back. It's as if he were waiting for her to return.

Get out of my mind, Rutherford. You left me and never returned the summer I left.

Maryanne realized she was creating more heartache for herself. She must forget Rutherford, but that kiss turned her inside out and upside down. Where did he learn to kiss like that? Even now it evoked feelings deep and hot. Her whole body was flushed in remembrance. Her pulsing heart missed him. Thank heavens he did not know. She was aching all over for him, and the flame was still high. All she can do was take a shower, but no, Liz would want to know what the matter was. She cannot admit she had sinned; that she had lust in her heart.

Eventually she must've fallen asleep because Liz was shaking her to wake up.

"You are talking in your sleep again."

"It's nothing. It's a recurring nightmare."

"Okay, sweetie, but let me tell you. The way you are fighting and thrashing about tells me there's something unresolved. You always scream no, no, and ask Rutherford to help you. What do you want rescued from? And don't say nothing!"

"I am sorry I disturbed your sleep. Really, I am," said Maryanne.

"Cut it! You know that's not the issue, Maryanne. You are like a sister to me. It's obvious something happened. Why do you think I threatened and dragged you to Jamaica!? I thought you needed a break from whatever disturbs your nights. I hoped you'd be relaxed and that you'd be infused with the Jamaican atmosphere; you'd leave those ghosts behind. Know you can ask for help. I am here. I am not going anywhere. Whatever is in my power, I'll do. Pray, fasting, talking whatever you ask," said Liz softly.

A week after the phone call, Maryanne started to exercise for two hours so she could be exhausted and go to bed. She woke Liz up three other times since their talk. It seemed the more she tried to suppress what happened, the more they came out at night. Liz didn't ask but quietly woke her but ruffled her hair. She's lucky to room with Liz. She was so soothing and pleasant. What she admired most was that she did not pry. She had several reasons to but refrains from doing so. Maryanne was shocked by how many times she talked in her sleep. She hoped Liz didn't think she's man-crazy. Why she was having all these nightmares. It was all legit, bonafide nightmares.

Four hyenas raped her and reversed her life forever. Yes. She had come a long way. She remembered when bile used to back up in her throat until she could not swallow. Resentment coursed through her veins. Even now, two years later, she was still angry. They bragged about raping her on one hand and then denied it when they were tried. And she was still fighting for sleep.

In October, the German students celebrate Octoberfest. Liz was not sure she wanted to attend as she had to double up on the Nurse Practitioner classes. Maybe she should slow down on the work because it was so intense. She was grateful she could wake Maryanne and go back to sleep, or she would be a zombie for lack of sleep. She encouraged Maryanne to go out with her study group, as she had assignments and papers to hand in. She wanted all As. She wanted the European tour her fiancée promised her for her honeymoon. She could inhale Paris, smell Venice, and was already on the gondolas. Liz worked from 4:30 p.m. to 11:30 p.m. that night. She completed all the assignments, read and made notes, and tomorrow would finish the paper. There was only one more paper after this. She cannot wait for graduation. She was not sure that she would march. She wanted to get back to her chocolate teddy, Zane. She missed him so much. She could not wait to write that final paper, sit both finals, and if she never saw another book, it wouldn't be too soon.

"Thank you, God, you brought me through. Couldn't have done it without you. Bless your holy name. Amen and Amen!" She turned off the light and slept immediately.

Maryanne opened the door, and Liz asked if everything was okay and fell asleep without hearing the answer. Maryanne went to the shower. Everything was fine until those boys started circling them on their bikes. The one in the red shirt was obnoxious. Though not violent by nature, she could have punched him. It was only after she raised her voice for him not to touch her that they backed off. Maybe the group would not go out with her again. Some men think they have license to touch a female. She was going to make sure to find mace and wear cargo pants so she'd not be encumbered with a pocketbook. That's easier because both hands were free.

Maryanne was awakened by Liz's voice urging her to wake up. "You are fighting in your sleep again and shouting 'don't touch me!'" She started to sob, and Liz hugged her and put her head on her shoulder. After she quieted down, Liz got up, and she asked Liz to stay with her. She just needed the comfort of her mother, but Liz will do.

Liz held her till she fell asleep. They awoke late the next morning, but thankfully it's Saturday and there were no classes for either.

"Last night," Maryanne said, "I just needed to feel safe and secure."

"I understand that. But you know it's not going to go away like that without you getting someone who can help professionally. Later, you may need a support group. That pain and anger will consume you. You are too fine a person to be consumed by this."

"You don't know!" said Maryanne.

"So why don't you tell. Correct the conclusions I have drawn."

"I can't. You don't understand," said Maryanne.

"Why? I'm not from a first-world country? Imagine! I'm an RN registered in an accelerated Master's and NP program, and I couldn't possibly know or understand anything you are going through? Really! Something traumatic happened to you and you are rehearsing over and over in your mind. You can't go on like this. The courses will get more challenging. I am not going to be comfortable leaving you alone," said Liz.

"You have been so supportive, Liz. Understanding, not pushy, and not once have you raised your voice. I have something to tell you." She drank half her orange juice. "I was raped," she said.

"Oh, my Lord, no! Oh no. Sweet Jesus, I am so sorry, pumpkin. That's the worst violation. You poor girl. Lord have mercy. Jesus, give my sister peace. I wish I could take this pain away from you. I am so very, very sorry. Oh, my sweet, no one deserves to be raped. Father God, your word said ask and it shall be given thee, and I am asking you do not forget the bastards. Let your wrath be poured out upon them tenfold. Continue to strengthen my sister Maryanne and give her healing from above."

All this time Liz had her arms wrapped around Maryanne, and tears rolled unchecked down her cheeks. She rocked Maryanne for both their sakes. Liz cannot think of anything to soothe her or take away the taint and stain from Maryanne. Little things she found strange made sense now. The way she rushed from the mirror, always touching her left eye, her cynical attitude towards Christianity and the church. It all added up. Poor Maryanne. The horror! The violation!

"It's a horrible thing that happened to you. The offenders got away from criminal justice but will not escape heavenly justice. Second Chronicles twenty verse fifteen says you should not be afraid of the great army because the battle is not yours but God's. Believe God is not done with you yet. I don't know why He allowed it to happen, but the perpetrators had a choice."

As the friends cried together, Liz encouraged her. Yes, it's going to be difficult to trust and believe, but she was a survivor. She told of the indomitable spirit of man. She would hold her head high again. There's nothing to be ashamed of. She did nothing wrong. As hard as it seemed, God would get you through this. She was sure she had come a long way and she should build on that.

"Continue in therapy! Street wisdom says the best revenge is to live well. Do that pumpkin. Remember Helen Reddy's 'Woman,' embrace the whole song or part of it. 'You Can Bend but Never Break Me' or 'I Am Woman Hear Me Roar.' Be defiant to your pain. You are stronger than you think. And remember, your safe haven, Jamaica, is an hour and a half away. Your family will pick you up," said Liz

After that talk with Liz, Maryanne felt new life breathing into her situation. She felt strong and empowered. She might seek help but will take Liz's advice. She would be defiant. She would not allow anything to control her. She continued to love Rutherford and did not want to give him up. She knew now he loved her, and it was her pride that pushed him away. She rationalized that who wanted the love of their life to see them at their worst. Maybe she was overthinking this. She always thought God was especially kind to men with high cheekbones, gorgeous eyes, raven-black curly hair, an athletic body, no fat, only flat abs. She smiled; this would certainly get her in a funk if she continued to daydream about Rutherford, who might have moved on already because she had cut him off. Oh well! Thanks, Liz! What her therapist said for all those months was reinforced by one session with Liz. Maybe she was just ready to hear. Thank God, out of the evil he provided her with an excellent extended family.

As per Liz's advice, she went to Student Affairs and her Academic Advisor. She listened to the suggestions and took the brochure. She expressed a desire for someone local on campus as long as no student works in the office. The recommendation was off-campus, five blocks away. This was funded through the school's student insurance. She found this more comfortable. She wanted no one outside of Liz to know. She saw Dr. Gwen Britton biweekly.

Maryanne was concerned about Liz's leaving. In another four months, she left. Tempted though she was, resisted the urge to spend Christmas in Jamaica, having to think of Felix. She could abandon him. She had a wonderful time in Jamaica, and that could be what she would share when she went home. Her study group was really working well; consequently, she rode with Sherry and boyfriend to Fort Lauderdale. They would stay overnight at the Marriott, and her mom would pick her up from there. Felix would be with her. She admitted that she was excited to see Felix. His voice was so deep and rich. He now had bulging muscles. Now he was on the basketball team at Audrey Keller High across town, opting not to go to Chelseatta High as she did. He was quiet-ish but not a fool. He remembered his sister's pain at that school.

Maryanne was happy to be home. She was bursting with excitement. She missed her first family. She was armed with souvenirs and stories, and more stories of Jamaica to regale the family and friends. She showed off her Jamaican lingo to the amusement of Renee.

"Eh! What did you do with my friend? I want her back. Too many changes. You will transfer and be with us," said Renee.

It was a wonderful reunion. There's a marked change in her demeanor. She's more confident and comfortable thanks to Liz and Dr. Britton and earlier therapists. She got it now. And still, she didn't ask what she was dying to know. Was Rutherford home. She must call Grams. But would

Rutherford recognize her because of the change? Would it matter? She picked up the phone and called Grams. Maryanne, Yolanda, and Renee took a walk. Maryanne insisted they go by Chelseatta High. It was important to take back her life, and this site held bittersweet memories for her. In as much as she wanted to hate it, this was where she met the love of her life. They passed Uncle Verne's Pizza, but Maryanne only wanted the garlic knots. This was where she would ask Rutherford to buy them when he was coming to see her. Maryanne inhaled deeply, struggling just a bit. What did Liz say to be defiant about her pain? Control it—what happened didn't define her.

It was a harsh life lesson, harder still because the rapists were not punished. She amended the thought, not yet punished.

Rutherford was home. He immediately noticed the slight change. She explained the reconstruction of her eye socket and other repairs that were hidden behind her glasses. They drove to Fort Myers and Punta Gorda. They went to the park there and sat by the harbor. She always found Punta Gorda quaint but charming, especially by the museum. It seemed timeless or ageless and there's a tranquility to it despite hurricanes and storms. She was sure that those trees that offered shade were close to a hundred years old. They talked about school, and Maryanne was happy to report that by next semester she would focus more on clinicals and would soon get the AS/RN but would flow straight to the BSN. Rutherford was impressed by her positive, progressive plans. He was happy she's asserting herself. Good for her!

Invariably the conversation got personal. He wanted to know how she's doing, if she's still in therapy. Was therapy beneficial? Was she healing? She admitted she was healing from first therapy to now and tremendous help from Liz her roommate. Liz knew what happened and was now a regular mother hen. He heard about the trip to Jamaica and the upcoming one for Liz's wedding next June. They held hands and talked with some of the old ease they had before.

"Do you know, Maryanne, I've never stopped loving you? From the first day I saw you, I loved you. And though you pushed me away, I still do."

"Rutherford please! I don't want to think about that now," she said (but knew she was lying to herself).

"Why? Afraid because you love me too and you don't want to admit it? That you erected a barrier, an invisible wall between us. What happened was horrendous. I was so scared that day that I'd lose you, and then somehow I thought I'd let you down."

"No. Please don't say that. You didn't let me down. You were hit in the head—you could easily have died. You didn't let me down," she said with a breaking voice.

"So why am I sitting in the corner? Guess that's a mystery then. Let's go find the ducks and watch the crafts."

They fed the ducks peanuts and bread. They walked hand in hand. She enjoyed the leisurely stroll. They chipped stones off the water, counting the skips, and watched the gulls dive into the water. One day she would find a pier and go fishing, but she's not standing on that bridge. It was too risky. They ate cheeseburgers and ice cream. That was their picnic. After the meal, Rutherford snapped his fingers.

"I know you are afraid of me. Afraid to show you desire me as much as I do you."

That message was not hers, and she's not taking it. He sat up and turned her face to his.

"What are you doing?" said Maryanne.

"Looking to see how many times I am going to kiss you. You blink twice in ten seconds, it's a yes . . ."

"You are not kissing me, boy, you just had cheese," she said.

"So did you. What's the problem? You had cheese. I had cheese, so we share a like. We'd just be swapping cheese," he said, grinning.

"You know you are sick. Get away from me," she said.

"Okay. We are going to play a game. I'm going to pinch your nose with your mouth closed, and we will see how long you can hold your breath. Come on, don't be a spoilsport," he said.

He pinched her nose and started to count. As he reached ten, she opened her mouth for air. Quickly he swooped down on her, and his lips fastened to hers in an everlasting, long kiss. He was not satisfied with one or two. She heard a whimpering sound and realized that's coming from her. She was lost in these kisses. They were drugging and seductive, and it's a long time before he released her. Well, despite what her words said, her lips and body gave another answer. As her breathing slowed, he nibbled her earlobes, and his tongue traced the outer ear, then the tip went inside. By then she was at his mercy. She could stop him—she didn't want to. She was not sure, but the feeling that came over her left her craving his touch. As he unbuttoned her blouse and kissed her tenderly, she begged him to stop.

"No, Ford (his pet's name). We can't and we mustn't."

"Why not, for heaven's sake? I know you enjoyed it and don't deny it."

"I am not denying it, but I can't, not like this. Anyway, you are the only man who has ever tempted me," she said.

"I should hope so," he growled, and the tension left his face. "It's not you, Ford, it's me. It's just how I feel because of what happened. I feel—" (he cut her off)

"Dirty, used and unworthy and ashamed? How do I know? I read it. Shocked? My dear Maryanne, I love you; that has not changed. I think no less of you because of that. I can understand you are self-conscious, but never dirty, never used. My love is stronger than that. I love you with everything I have. I won't pressure you—I will wait for you to heal. No worry, when we do you will be wearing my ring. It's like Beres Hammond says: 'Each time you pass my way I'm tempted to touch,'" he said.

And he hugged her, and she felt safe. She was happy he understood, even though she didn't articulate that well.

The three friends had a wonderful Christmas vacation, with Ford joining them on many occasions. They chatted and laughed about campus life and the shenanigans of some of the students. College campuses were a regular melting pot. There were so many international students and accents, and the vastness of some campuses was quite unbelievable. It was easy to see why some lost their way. None of them hung out much with the partying crowd. Maryanne was happy for Liz's influence on her study life and life on campus. She was seriously thinking after next spring to enroll in the accelerated

BSN program. Soon they had to leave. Maryanne had one more flaming date with him today. She was missing him already. However, she was determined that she would not cry.

Epilogue

S o at long last, she had completed six years of study. She was an RN and an NP. She had three degrees: AS in Nursing, BSN in Nursing, and MS/ NP. Naturally, her Jamaican as well as her American family were present at the graduation. She had gained vast experience in nursing. After graduating with the BSN, she worked at Eastern Hospital in Orlando. It wasn't gigantic, but it was county, and she needed the experience. Within a year of getting her NP license, she was going to be on the road as a traveling nurse for a while. She had a mind to travel to Kansas and New Orleans. She wanted to visit friends Matthew Busch and Chad Broome. After all, she needed to thank them. They made it to the major league, and so did she. She's all woman now. She had changed enough that they would not recognize her. That first vacation she had in Jamaica gave her hips she never relinquished, but they were nice hips and her body was sleek and smooth. Her eyes were smoky and sultry. That's her new look. Woman on a mission!

The year was up, and it was football season. She bought a ticket. Here began phase one of Operation: The Return.

As the plane lifted off, Maryanne looked through the window as Orlando Airport receded. Her lips curled in a delicious smile, but the eyes remained blank. *Well, my nurse, how do you like me now?*

She switched to a flaming red head at Louis Armstrong Airport. She entered as a blonde and exited as a redhead. She hailed a cab.

"Tryall Cesare please …"